SIX

IN THE BED

D1360137

Most Perigee Books are available at special quantity discounts for bulk purchases for sales promotions, premiums, fund-raising or educational use. Special books, or book excerpts, can also be created to fit specific needs.

For details, write: Special Markets, The Berkley Publishing Group, 200 Madison Avenue, New York, New York 10016.

SIX
IN THE BED

Dealing with Parents, In-Laws, and
Their Impact on Your Marriage

Nancy Wasserman Cocola

A Perigee Book

HOUSTON PUBLIC LIBRARY

R01068 62463

A Perigee Book
Published by The Berkley Publishing Group
A member of Penguin Putnam Inc.
200 Madison Avenue
New York, NY 10016

Copyright © 1997 by Nancy Wasserman Cocola
Book design by Rhea Braunstein
Cover design by Charles Björklund
Cover illustration by Bonnie Timmons

All rights reserved. This book, or parts thereof, may not be reproduced
in any form without permission.

First edition: November 1997

Published simultaneously in Canada.

The Putnam Berkley World Wide Web site address is
http://www.berkley.com

Library of Congress Cataloging-in-Publication Data

Cocola, Nancy Wasserman.
Six in the bed : dealing with parents, in-laws, and their impact on
your marriage / Nancy Wasserman Cocola. — 1st ed.
p. cm.
"A Perigee book."
Includes bibliographical references.
ISBN 0-399-52343-X
1. Married people—United States—Psychology. 2. Married people—
United States—Family relationships. 3. Parent and adult child—United
States—Psychology. 4. Parents-in-law—United States—Family
relationships. I. Title.
HQ734.C5927 1997
306.87—dc21
96-53676
CIP

Printed in the United States of America

10 9 8 7 6 5 4 3 2 1

*For my mother
in memory, with love*

CONTENTS

ACKNOWLEDGMENTS

A special thank-you to my agent, Carla Glasser, whose keen eye for organization advanced this project at a critical juncture. As always, I am indebted to her for her support and encouragement.

My gratitude to my editor, Suzanne Bober, for her invaluable suggestions, her kind, collaborative spirit, and her efforts in bringing this book to light.

I would like to thank all the couples who have shared their lives with me over the past two decades. It is always my profound privilege to be allowed entree into such a private world.

Finally, deep love and thanks to my husband, John, and my son, Matt, who once again had ringside seats. Even in the midst of the fray, I could always hear them cheering for me.

Introduction

"A family's photograph album is generally about the extended family . . . and, often, is all that remains of it."
Susan Sontag[1]

You are nestled in your sofa, with a hot cup of cocoa, a wool throw draped across your lap, watching an old Western on television. You watch the heartening scenes of pioneers heading west in their Conestoga wagons—what more could you ask for on a rainy, cold fall day? Within those wagons rumbling across the open prairie, laden down with hopeful homesteaders, there was always Ma, Pa, the kids and as many relatives as could be crammed on board. Those were the good old days, when families faced all manner of danger and adventure together in order to make a new life. These are the images of family so romanticized by Hollywood, which still hold our hearts and resonate to many of us. These movie moments showed us how several generations could live side by side raising children and working the land together with common economic goals. These films even showed us the struggles between the generations for power, self-determination, and control. But most of all they showed us something that seems to be missing from modern family life: the willingness to endure and persevere in order to forge and maintain relationships with parents, in-laws, and grandparents. Certainly, for the pioneers, much of the willingness to do this was born out of necessity. People were needed in order to populate the growing towns. Many hands were needed to manage the family farm. Multigenerational homesteads were essential to help pass down skills and knowledge from one generation to another. This was survival. This was also the ethos of the times. Families overcame their conflicts and differences and surrounded themselves with love in the hostile environment of the uncharted West. Comfort was found within the family.

With the urbanization of America, the size of families diminished. Having many children to work the farm was no longer necessary. While young couples moved on to seek their fortune in the cities, parents and in-laws often were left back on the farm. But that ethos, that approach to family support and family sustenance, was also left behind. The industrial revolution valued independence and individual achievement, driving the concept of multigenerational family dominance into the background.

In the 1950s, suburbanization was all the rage. Young couples bought into the idea that their success was measured in terms of their earning power, independence, education, and ability to assimilate. Youthfulness was venerated, and the ideal family was touted as a home with 2.5 children, a mother, and a father. There was little room for parents and in-laws in this world. Anthropologist Margaret Mead commented on this dilemma in an article in the journal *New Realities*. "Nobody has ever before asked the nuclear family to live all by itself in a box the way we do. With no relatives, no support, we've put it in an impossible situation."[2]

Today we find families settling the final frontier. Globalization has reached into the family and changed the way we conceive of the all-important relationships on the family landscape. Children have moved away from their parents to live in other states, even other countries. Jobs, not family ties, frequently dictate where a couple will live. And by now, parents have caught on. They too are influenced by the concepts of mobility and independence. Sometimes they don't "stay put" either.

We've created a society of socially isolated families. Relations have been strained by distance, work and the "me" ethos of the past three decades. *Family Values* is a political phrase, but it cradles beneath its rhetoric a genuine yearning for a time when families were closer and the world was a smaller place. Couples have begun to feel a need to relearn the lost art of having a true involvement with their parents. They are moving their families back home to be closer to their folks in record numbers. At the same time we find parents and in-laws picking up roots and moving to be near their children as old age approaches. There are a myriad of reasons why these changes are taking place, and for each family they are unique. However, there are distinct social forces creating the need for these shifts. As economic necessity dictates that both parents work full-time jobs to make ends meet, we see families moving closer together to ostensibly secure grandparent baby-sitters. Many couples are finding themselves in financial straits and requiring aid from parents from whom they may well have been independent for some time. For some, the sole reason for moving closer together is so children can feel the delight of knowing their grandparents. And finally, parents live longer now, which means couples are having to discover ways to meet new and growing family obligations.

Learning how to have the longed-for relationship with their parents and in-laws while maintaining the integrity of their marriage can be the greatest challenge in a couple's married life. Parents play such an enormous part in the shaping, supporting, or leveling of a marriage. Whether they do this with a roar or a whisper, from distant climes or from right next door, their influence can be felt in every marriage. As couples reach for increased emotional connection or actual physical proximity to their parents and in-laws, they must learn to guide these relationships. Plenty of skeptics believe that close relationships with parents are impossible. "Why bother to move closer?" they say. "Why not take the promotion and stay in Japan for another two years? The phone is as close as we want to get to that emotional hornets' nest." Unfortunately, there really is no choice. You may opt for the Orient, but the influences of your parents' marriages took the same 747 and arrived along with all your other baggage when you reached Tokyo.

We can take comfort in knowing that not only humans have parent and in-law problems. The female white-breasted bee-eater in Kenya has a father-in-law who could throw a monkey wrench into the workings of any marriage. Once his young son leaves the nest to start his own family, the father will begin daily, friendly visits to the bride and groom. Delightful as his demeanor may be (chirping happily and playfully darting around), his goal is to interfere, to make it difficult for the new couple to feather their nest. He will attempt to manipulate and sweet-talk his son into returning home to help care for his own new clutch of babes. Ultimately, he forces his young son to leave his new wife alone at home on their nest, struggling to raise her own brood. In fact, a 1992 study of white-breasted bee-eaters by Drs. Emlen and Wrege of Cornell University has shown that forty percent of the time, the new bee-eater groom will abandon his wife and cede to the coercion of his father.[3] Our indignation surfaces toward the interfering father-in-law, and we have nothing but disdain for the weak-winged groom who couldn't say no and remain on the nest to help his new wife.

But, how many of us can say with impunity that we have *always* made choices that were in the best interests of our marriage and that we've resisted the subtle and not so subtle pressure brought to bear by our parents? How many of us have consumed *two* Thanksgiving dinners because we didn't know how to say no to two sets of pleading parents? How many times have you fought with your spouse, or suffered long evenings of smoldering rage, as your spouse planned yet another fishing weekend with his dad, or a shopping spree with her mom, without discussing it with you first? Whenever a couple takes on the challenge of having a real, hands-on relationship with their parents, they need the tools with which to be able to identify and modulate their parents' sphere of influence. They must uncover and dismantle the emotional land mines that such closeness often hides within it. Dr. Lee Salk may have said it best in his book *Family-hood*: "Frustration with your family may make you want to scream, but it also challenges you to learn to be more diplomatic, to find ways of minimizing the frustration and stresses, to learn the hard but worthwhile lessons of patience and tolerance."[4]

Throughout this book, couples will be taught how to identify, modify, and choose the way in which their parents will influence their marriage. The first lesson a couple must learn is that simply watching their parents' marriage over the years has informed them as individuals. Then they must observe how that influence gets played out in their own marriage.

The first section, "The Marriage Mirror," offers couples a peek into the looking glass to see how their parents' marriage reflects their own. They will see how their *expectations* of their own marriage are often a mirror image of how their parents' marriage took shape. Here too, couples will learn how their role in their original family, whether Peacemaker or Rebel, Indulged Child or Caretaker, plays an important part in how they end up shaping their interactions with their spouse.

Section Two is appropriately called "Renegotiating Attachments," for this is one of the principal tasks facing a couple in the early years of their marriage. But take heart! If you are a middle-aged couple reading this book, and you still haven't gotten this right, there is still hope. This skill can be learned any time, and it is never too late to use it. These chapters introduce the true power in marriage, the concept of the "Royal We." It points out the natural resistance that surfaces as a couple attempts to realign themselves. This section offers specific skills that can be used on a daily basis.

Section Three, "The Marriage Sampler," is designed topically to allow couples easy access to specific dilemmas they may be facing, and provides alternative scenarios using the skills discussed in previous chapters. So if your mother-in-law is threatening to withhold your son's school tuition if he doesn't also attend religious training classes three times a week, and you have smoke coming out of your ears after arguing with her for an hour on the phone, you can flip to the chapter called "Dollars and Common Sense" for a quick glimpse at ways to handle that or a similar situation. And if your father-in-law has just moved into your home after the death of your mother-in-law, you can turn to the chapter called "Aging Parents—Family Helping Family."

Consider for a moment that parent and in-law problems are ranked among the top complaints that couples face in their married life. Consider too the good news that with the proper information, skills, and guidance, a couple can bring these pressures on their marriage down to a minimum. You will no longer feel the urge to hide in a closet until your in-laws' visit is over. You and your spouse will no longer have to get into fruitless battles in which you attack each other's flawed and faulty excuse for parents. You will be able to anticipate events and dilemmas before they arise. You will know how to reach a consensus and raise your concerns in a productive, judicious manner. The clarity and unity you will be building with your spouse will make it possible to see your parents and in-laws as allies instead of adversaries. No longer will they be the enemies crossing the border, but rather invited ambassadors who will come on visits satisfying to both nations.

Learning to navigate the tricky terrain of your familial relationships can invigorate your marriage. In these pages, you will learn how to attain a sense of power, humor, and adulthood—while maintaining and building positive working and loving relationships with your parents and in-laws.

The Marriage Mirror

CHAPTER ONE

Reflections

*"The Image is more than an idea. It is a vortex or
cluster of fused ideas and is endowed with energy."*
Ezra Pound[5]

Everyone learns how to be married by watching the marriages around them. Whether you spent your time absorbing a "good" marriage, or being buffeted by the effects of your parents' "bad" marriage, it is essential that you look at how those influences come to bear on your own marriage.

Amy considered her parents' marriage a good one. She tells of how her parents have a wonderful union; they do absolutely everything together. She had always assumed that her marriage would involve this kind of togetherness. She, however, was married to Richard, not her father. Richard was an inquisitive, diverse, and happy man. He has a list of things he wants to do and carries it around in his wallet. He has some interests that he considers solitary, such as painting. He also is a member of a men's bowling league. And though he spends lots of time with Amy, it never seems to be enough. They fight over his "independence" and her feelings of abandonment.

Nina's parents were so estranged that they hardly ever spoke. Their idea of a conversation was a series of two-word sentences jotted down on the kitchen notepad. When she married Sal, she couldn't believe her good luck. He was a talkative and communicative guy who adored her. He, however, spent long hours at his job, often returning home after she had gone to sleep and leaving before she awoke. He took to writing her little notes on the kitchen notepad. His notes, filled with love and instructions or information for the day ahead, drove her into a frenzy of rage. Sal returned home early one evening to find Nina ready to argue with him about the "demands" he was making in his little notes that he left her. What did he mean by leaving her "instructions" to take his shirts to the cleaner and make sure his shoes were soled? Sal didn't understand what he was doing wrong, and Nina wasn't clear either. She didn't mind running those errands for Sal. It was the notes that were driving her crazy. If Nina and Sal don't take a look into the Marriage Mirror, they may never understand the argument they are having.

Trying to duplicate your parents' "good" marriage, or attempting to cast off any behaviors reminiscent of your parents' "troubled" marriage, usually doesn't work. But couples can take a look at their parents' style of marriage and understand how their parents' relationship has influenced their own. This knowledge and perspective can shed much light on the way a couple interacts with each other—and with their parents. The Marriage Mirror reflects all of this information. A couple need only take the time to recognize the reflections that they see etched there. Then they can take that information and apply it to their marriage in a way that informs and enlightens their behavior.

Great Expectations

In past generations, traditions guided couples as they embarked on their marital journey. Years could pass without any changes being made in the way holidays were celebrated, births were announced, deaths were acknowledged, and male and female roles were played out. Each couple had a kind of marital road map in their back pockets and knew how the journey was supposed to go. Today, people are marrying outside their social, economic, and religious groups. Many of the old rules don't apply. They are taking on new tasks and roles. Options are abundant. Instead of following historically established routes through marriage, they must see how they can join their own diverse origins to become a true working original.

Frank, a young executive, related this story:

"I got to my office after lunch and there was a voice mail message from my wife. It said, 'Meet me at Mom and Dad's for dinner . . . 7 o'clock.' This was the third Friday night in a row that we were going there for dinner. I had been looking forward to kicking off my shoes, having dinner alone with my wife, and letting nature take its course. How did I get roped into this every Friday night thing?"

This couple is about to get their first glimpse into the Marriage Mirror—and see how their parents' marital style and expectations have influenced their own.

Frank's wife, Mindy, simply took it for granted that when she got married, she would spend her Friday nights at her parents' house. Her family had always had Friday night dinner with Mindy's grandparents. There was a *generational expectation*—a tradition, if you will. Mindy never really thought about it; she simply expected to take part in it. The first time she ever gave it any thought was the Friday she found herself sitting on the edge of the sofa as Frank stood over her yelling that he hated going to her folks' house, while she cried, "We've always done it this way!"

Frank and Mindy hadn't, up until now, looked into the

Marriage Mirror. Mindy expected to carry on a family tradition. Frank had no such expectation. He had never experienced regular family dinners and consequently had no family expectations of this sort to bring to the marriage. How can these two reflections be modified so this couple can have a peaceful Friday night every now and again?

Both Sides Now . . . The Art of Reframing

On the face of it, Mindy saw Frank as being obstinate and withholding. Why couldn't he give in on just this little thing? Was it too much to ask? If he *really* loved her, he would understand what these dinners meant to her. Frank saw Mindy as being too weak to say no to her parents and give him the time he deserved as her husband. Why couldn't she give in on just this little thing? After all, they saw her parents plenty of other times. If she *really* loved him, she would understand and want a quiet night at home with him at the end of the week. They let each other know this in no uncertain terms in a heated debate that left each of them feeling completely misunderstood by the other.

What if the couple looked at the events of that Friday night with a new slant? What if Mindy reframed or redefined Frank's wish to be alone with her as complimentary and wonderful? What if Frank reframed Mindy's wish to go to her family every Friday night as keeping a tradition of family closeness alive for yet another generation? Neither one is out to deprive the other of anything. Neither one means to hurt the other. What woman wouldn't want her husband to express a hankering to be with her? What man wouldn't want a wife who values tradition and a warm family? From the positive vantage point of reframing, each was able to see the other's viewpoint more readily. They hit upon a compromise that, though not exactly equal, gave hope and room for further discussion. They decided that three out of four Fridays they would dine with Mindy's folks, and on the fourth Friday they would stay home together. It seems like a small change, but it was difficult to effect. Mindy had much anxiety explaining to her parents their decision for the Friday off, and breaking with the generational expectation. Frank, though happier, would have liked even more time with Mindy. However, it was a start.

When a couple looks in the Marriage Mirror, they have the opportunity to assess where they came from and modify where they are heading. They have a chance to redefine or reframe aspects of the relationship they see as negative, but are really just imprints from the marriages that have gone before them. In order to cast their own reflection in the Marriage Mirror, they may need to look again at what they see and redefine it. By reframing, a family begins to find new ways to look at things through a common lens in order to advance their health and sense of unity. The same need arises for couples. They must begin to look at each other's behavior not as malevolent machinations, but as the positive expression of longing.

Good Fences Make Good Neighbors

The reflections of the Marriage Mirror go well beyond family dinners. They encompass all the expectations, hopes, behaviors, and beliefs a couple brings to their marriage. At their parents' knees they learn to fight, to love, and to resolve conflict. They learn how decisions are made and who has the power in the marriage. From watching their parents and grandparents interact, they learn the difference between help and interference. They learn what can be overlooked and what constitutes a marital call to arms.

Gregory grew up in a family where things were run by committee. He was used to seeing the door to his house thrown open as uninvited relatives swept in, hugged and kissed each other hello, and convened at the kitchen table to discuss the day's news and gossip. He was used to such behavior. Gregory's wife, Pat, was from a family in which people called before they showed up, in which there was a kind of formal sense of space. There was not a lot of kissing or hugging, not a lot of *interference*. These were the reflections they saw in the Marriage Mirror.

Yet when Pat married Greg, it was his family that attracted her to him—their warmth, his mother's ever-brewing pot of coffee and the affection she received at his parents' house. She never really noticed how much the family discussions were peppered with directives to "help" her run her household. Now years into her marriage, she was becoming disenchanted with all that had once drawn her to them. For reasons unclear to Greg, Pat was spending less and less time with the family, making excuses for not visiting and walking around disgruntled and annoyed much of the time.

No longer a young bride, Pat had the confidence to run her life without the benefit of a committee, and was beginning to experience some appreciation for her own family's more hands-off style. In fact, she was finding out that she rather liked a bit of formal distance. She liked the idea of inviting people over rather than having them always show up at inopportune times. Just as the invasion of Greg's family was odious to Pat, Greg couldn't grasp why her family was so distant and formal. They seemed abnormal to him. He kept arguing that his family always "meant well." Indeed, he was right about that. All their suggestions were coming from a place of love. The fact that Pat was beginning to be irritated by "so much loving intent" was hard for him to fathom. She kept saying that her family had more respect for them as a couple and had more faith in them to make their own decisions. The arguments began small and escalated to character assassinations of relatives on both sides. What to do?

Finding Neutral Ground

Some people think of boundaries as negative things. They associate them with keeping others away and being isolated.

It's hard to comprehend how the term got such a miserable reputation. Countries have borders, farms have stone walls, rooms have doors, and generations have boundaries. These walls and boundaries merely offer an opportunity for those within to have some measure of autonomy. Within these boundaries families can express themselves freely, can find comfort and be assured that they can conduct their affairs as they see fit. The beauty of a boundary is that it always has points of entry. Every border has checkpoints for access and egress. Every stone wall has places to allow the hay cart and cows through. Every generational boundary has spaces through which people are welcomed within to offer help, advice and love. The hard part about creating family boundaries is that they aren't mandated by law and aren't visible. By looking in the Marriage Mirror, however, a couple can get a picture of where the generational boundaries were permeable in their parents' marriages. Then they can decide where they are willing to place their own doorways.

The families of Pat and Greg had absolutely opposite views on boundaries. It was only after they came together to discuss the fact that one family simply had more boundaries than the other, and that neither held a premium on the right way to build those boundaries, that they began to redefine and reframe their arguments. Once they reframed Pat's wish for control over her own household as a positive desire, rather than an act designed to hurt Greg's family, they began to move from argument to agreement, from conflict to consensus.

Now, how can a couple find neutral ground? It's an act of will; there is no other way to describe it. Agreement must be reached, with compromise and mutual respect as the guiding tenets. Since a change in their attitude and behavior would affect Greg's family, Pat and Greg had to move slowly and gingerly to find an approach to talking with them and expressing themselves clearly. A discussion of how a couple can effectively communicate these issues to their families is included in Section Two: "Renegotiating Attachments." This section explains how to present information to families and meet and beat your resistance as a couple to doing the things that will improve the situation.

Government by the People and for the People

Every decision in the Winchester household was made by Tim. At first, Anna thought that his interest in the flowers for their wedding, the tile for the new bathroom, the style of the children's shoes, and the color of the henna rinse she used to cover her increasingly graying hair was wonderful. At last, a truly involved man. In the beginning of their married life, Anna had enjoyed the shelter she found in Tim's decisive manner and seeming interest in everything relating to her and the children. She had always felt uneasy when she had to make decisions on her own. She was forever second-guessing herself and changing her mind. Tim came into her life and relieved her of all her self-doubt, and she willingly agreed to their arrangement.

Lately that positive definition had fallen by the wayside, and Anna saw only Tim's controlling, manipulative, and demanding nature. Her quest to take back some of the responsibilities from Tim, which was a commendable plan, was causing friction and disillusionment. She had tried the "one person, one vote" approach with Tim, but it never seemed to get her anywhere. One of her friends had recently commented, "So who promised you that marriage was going to be a democracy?" Anna thought more frequently about leaving him and being her own person, on her own. What to do?

Checks and Balances

Mirror, mirror on the wall, whose decision counts after all? If Tim and Anna stop for a moment and look in the Marriage Mirror, they will find what they need to begin to solve this problem. Anna has always seen her marriage as the reverse of her own parents' relationship. It was always her mother who decided everything, with her father operating as a shadowy, benevolent figure who "allowed her to have her way." Anna had been told for as long as she could remember that she was just like her father. She did have a special affection for him, and he for her. They shared the same large hands and hazel eyes. Tim, on the other hand, looks in the mirror and sees his father dominating every family discussion and shaping every family decision. He can even hear his father saying, "A man takes the wheel and sets the course for the whole family." His father loved sailing and imagined himself the commodore and the family his crew!

Once Tim and Anna got to talking about the past, they were able to express their feelings about their parents' arrangements. Anna had always felt that she could rely on her mother, but secretly felt bad that her father didn't take a more decisive role in the family. In fact, she had always harbored a bit of anger at him for not standing up to her mother. Tim, on the other hand, always regarded his father as a bit of a good-natured bully, and though he respected him, he often felt squelched by him as he watched his mother live a life of quiet, passive acceptance.

In discussing this with Anna, Tim got a glimpse of himself as a well-meaning bully and it upset him, but he also had strong associations with decision-making and manhood. Anna saw how being like her father was making her angry with herself for not speaking up more. Her anger at Tim was really a reflection of her past anger at her dad and at herself. Once this dialogue was opened, they were able to talk about how they didn't want their marriage to reflect their parents' in this area of decision making. So, they hit on the idea of a more democratic union; a system of checks and balances. For now Tim will remain President, but Anna has taken on the role of Majority Leader in the Senate. She has the power and the mandate to lobby to overturn a decision when the President makes a judgment that the Senator feels is not in the best interest of the family. She also has the job of voicing the opinions of her constituency (the children) should the President overstep their rights as well.

And they've met with their own resistance. You'll find out more about that in Chapter Five. Tim found it hard to keep from jumping in every time Anna exercised her rights. Anna found it difficult to stick to her guns if she was questioned. However, had they not taken a look into the Marriage Mirror, they would not have had the information necessary to begin to tackle this problem.

Money Makes the World Go Round

Mike Watson was a hardworking man, and his wife, Carla, was known affectionately around town as the tag sale expert and village spendthrift. All of this had gone on for years, as their house filled up with bric-a-brac and objets d'art that no other resident of their town wanted. Mike looked upon his wife's spending with a tolerance that could only be described as paternal. Carla was a delightful and tireless woman who maintained a beautiful home and did a lot for their four very energetic children. She could be seen ferrying them from soccer to ballet to karate and late into the night could be found sewing curtains for the girls' room, checking homework, and making lunches for the next day.

But their situation changed when Mike's job as chief quality control inspector at the GM plant was cut in what proved to be the first of many layoffs in their community. Because he had seniority, he was offered another job for less pay. With jobs being scarce and his benefits and retirement package being all tied up at the plant, he accepted. Money was suddenly an issue when it never had been before. Mike was tense and worried. Their savings were almost nonexistent, and Mike talked about the family living more conscientiously on a budget. Carla agreed, but then found herself at

a tag sale on Sunday buying beanbag chairs and three antique carpet beaters to hang up "somewhere" in the house;
she wasn't exactly sure where. Mike blew his stack when he
saw her emptying out the back of their ten-year-old station
wagon. How was it she couldn't get it through her head that
they had a serious problem on their hands? What was she,
a child? The kids had accepted the situation better than she
had. What to do?

Centsible Solutions

One quick look in the Marriage Mirror made things blind-
ingly clear to both Carla and Mike. Mike's parents were
divorced, and though his mother worked, her job didn't provide enough money for them to live. Child support payments
were often late, and there was always an underlying tension
in their house about the type of man their father was, to play
such games and be so selfish with his money. Mike's mother
forfeited many things so that her children would be provided
for. Their home was sparsely furnished, and she had just
enough clothing for the work week. Mike and his brother,
however, always seemed to have opportunities to play on
sports teams, have new clothes for school, and even have
enough pocket money to take girls out when they became
old enough. Mike and his brother always felt embarrassed
by their home and their mother, who wore the same house-
dress around the house, even after it was faded from so much
washing. They never felt comfortable inviting their friends
over after school. Guilt about those feelings came rushing
over Mike as he described those early days of struggle to
Carla. Though his mother's situation is more comfortable
now, Mike finds himself buying his mom new things that
she won't buy for herself.

Carla's glance in the mirror found a family with little or
no money for any extras. The family moved often to accom-
modate her father's endless search for steady work. No place
they lived ever really resembled a home. After so many years

of moving and disappointment, her mother had given up trying. Carla's parents fought frequently about the issue of money and debt. Carla never had extra shoes, extra clothes, or pocket money. Never having had any discretionary money to play with, she never learned how to manage money. One of the things that was a great source of pride for Carla was that she and Mike didn't fight over money and that her home really was just that: a comfortable, inviting haven for her family.

Mike hadn't quite remembered all this about Carla. They really hadn't discussed their pasts since their days of courtship, when every vital piece of information about themselves was shared and cherished. He had forgotten how potent her past had been in shaping her identity. He also began to realize why he had kept so quiet about her spendthrift ways until now. He hadn't wanted to see her deprived as his mother had been. He couldn't have withstood a life of more guilt over money. Mike also realized that Carla provided him with something he always wanted: a home he could be proud of, where he could bring people and feel good. Carla now understood Mike's "generosity of spirit" when it came to her spending. She also began to see that she was no longer that bereft little girl. She had what she wanted and needed. Also, she began to see that her children were growing up in a completely different environment than she had and did not need more things to feel secure.

Unfortunately, she still didn't know how to manage money, and their solution had to address that problem. At a family powwow they all decided to take an allowance, from the youngest child to the oldest adult. That amount had to last the entire week for each of them. They functioned only with cash and kept the checkbook and credit cards put away on a closet shelf. Physical emergencies or household repairs were the only times they could be used. A few times Carla used up her allowance at a Sunday tag sale and had no other funds for the rest of the week. Once or twice, Mike spent his allowance on a frivolous item for Carla that he purchased during one of his "guilty moments." Overall, however, they worked together to dispel the old reflections and realize that the reflection of their marriage didn't resemble the ones of their parents. Though Mike was making less money than before, it didn't mean that they were suddenly a deprived family. The glimpse into the Marriage Mirror refreshed long-forgotten bits of their past that were still informing the way in which their marriage was being conducted.

Though the Marriage Mirror can't always provide you with an immediate solution to problems, it can begin a dialogue. By looking in you are also recognizing the power that resides in the model of marriage your parents provided. Good, bad, or indifferent, their image is forever etched on the very same mirror on which you are now casting your own marital reflection. As a first step to modifying the impact your parents' marriage has upon your own, the Marriage Mirror is invaluable. As a place you go routinely to look when you and your spouse are in conflict, the Marriage Mirror is essential. And, as a source of mutual understanding and respect, the Marriage Mirror is brimming with hope and possibility. The Marriage Mirror is a multifaceted item. Not only can you see your parents' marriages in it, but you can see the role you were given in your family of origin. It will bring to light how the reflection of these roles, long designated and played out in your original family, is a potent predictor of the role you will instinctively take on in your marriage and with your new family. In the next chapter, we'll take a look at these specific roles, which will add to the knowledge you have already gleaned through examining your reflection in the Marriage Mirror.

CHAPTER TWO

Roles Couples Play

Everybody grows up with a designated role they play in their family of origin. The eldest child may be a parent's *Confidant*. A particularly sensitive child may have become the family *Peacemaker* who actively works to keep calm in the family. Still others may have been the *Rebels*, and were expected to have their own minds and do their own thing. When a couple gets married, they bring to their relationship these roles, which they have been perfecting since birth. For couples, these roles are often perfect emotional fits. A Peacemaker and a Rebel, for instance, "feed" each other's long-designated roles in ways that are often satisfying and comfortable for both of them. But when outside pressure from family heightens their roles in a way that is uncomfortable for the couple, it can create tension in the couple's private interactions and in their ongoing relationship with their parents.

Rebel and Peacemaker

Carol, a wife, mother, and office manager, came to her marriage with the designated role of Peacemaker. She got her on-the-job training from her mother, who always tried to smooth the feathers of her often ruffled father. Her mother worked hard to keep her husband's volatile temper from affecting the kids and embarrassing them in front of the neighbors and other family. No better teacher could have been available to Carol. Her mother was the master when it came to peacemaking.

Rick, on the other hand, was the Rebel in his family of origin. He was the only boy, born to a buttoned-down, toe-the-line kind of father and a delightfully ineffective mother who could never get him to do what she wanted him to do. Though his behavior as an adolescent had caused his parents a lot of concern, and they always seemed to be in some conflict or other, Rick always felt that his dad got a secret kick out of his rebellious ways and envied him his ability to do his own thing. As he had gotten older, he had found more appropriate ways of being his own man, and when he married Carol, his mother heaved a sigh of relief that he was settling down and taking on responsibility. Maybe Carol could get him to do the right thing.

Carol reported a dilemma that reflected how the role she perfected while living with her own family of origin powerfully affected her relationship with Rick—and got her caught in an impasse with her mother-in-law:

"My mother-in-law and I have always gotten along. My real problems only exist when she tries to get to Rick through me. We had a family wedding to go to; Rick's sister's, in fact. Being asked to be an usher meant Rick had to wear a tuxedo. My husband doesn't even own a suit, so you can imagine the fuss he put up about the tux. He was willing to forego the honor of being an usher just to avoid the confines of a tuxedo. Never mind that his mother was hysterical or his sister might be upset, this is Rick. I've learned what Rick will and won't do. He's a great guy . . . just has his own mind."

Carol had, over the years, made peace with Rick's style, and though at times she may not have loved how he chose to do something, she was such a Peacemaker at heart that she would find a way of smoothing it over in her own mind and in the eyes of others. Rick also had mellowed over the years. He had children and responsibilities that he took seriously, so his rebellious streak usually came out concerning issues he felt were not threatening to the well-being of his kids or his wife. But this situation was different. Carol was no longer dealing with just herself and Rick. Rick's mother had entered into the equation and was bringing pressure to bear on Carol to perform what she herself had never been able to do with Rick—get him to go along with what the family wanted:

"My mother-in-law called every day for updates on my success or failure in getting Rick to acquiesce. Well, there I was in the middle. I felt so much pressure that we fought over that damn tux until I wasn't sure if we'd be going to a family wedding or getting a divorce."

Her first problem, of course, was that she was fighting with her husband more and more as she felt squeezed between his rebellious style, his mother's wish to head off the problem before Rick's father got wind of his obstinacy, and her own need to keep peace and please her mother-in-law. She wanted Rick to comply with his family's wishes, and she wanted her mother-in-law to stop expecting her to change her son. She wanted to get out of the middle of this impossible situation! In her designated role as Peacemaker, she felt it was unfeasible for her to tell this to her mother-in-law directly. Rick's designated role had always made it impossible for him to give in on these types of things. What to do?

Instead of going through one more knockout round of arguing, Carol and Rick needed to take a look into the Marriage Mirror. When they looked, they saw the legacy of the roles they were asked to play. Carol saw why she was so angry with Rick. Rick was acting just like her own father: hostile, unpredictable, and potentially a source of embarrassment to the family at the wedding. Her anger was compounded by the pressure she felt from her mother-in-law to act on her behalf, to change the boy that she herself had never been able to change.

Rick glimpsed into the mirror and realized why he was so angry with Carol. She was acting on behalf of his family, attempting to change his ways and siding with the "establishment" on this issue. He didn't need anyone telling him what to do at this late date in his life. His anger at Carol was reminiscent of how he used to feel as an adolescent when dealing with his ineffective mother. And he was treating Carol just like he had treated his mother: with contempt and anger.

For Rick and Carol, the Rebel/Peacemaker roles had been a perfect fit. Indeed, they would continue to be for years to come, so long as they could modify the effect that Rick's family had of intensifying these roles whenever they wanted something from Rick. Rick would jump into overdrive and turn into the recalcitrant adolescent, and Carol would intensify her peacemaking efforts to such a pitch that she could have won the Nobel Peace Prize had anyone from the Nobel committee been paying attention!

An immediate solution was for Carol to step aside and allow Rick to deal with his mother directly, and Rick needed to take more responsibility for the decision he was making. He was going on with his daily routine while the women around him were tap-dancing on the head of a pin, hoping he would see the light and give in. By nicely directing her mother-in-law to speak to Rick every time she asked about the tuxedo problem, Carol was freeing herself from being the one responsible for the success of the campaign, and from being the one to hear her mother-in-law's worry. By having Rick deal directly with his mother and sister, she was also permitting him to see and feel their distress with him firsthand—and she wasn't absorbing it. *She* would be free of her anger at him for putting her in such a position. *He* would be taking the heat for his own decisions. By looking into the Marriage Mirror, they were able to identify the seeds of their frustration with each other, and begin to think of "doing their marriage differently."

In Section Two, you will be shown how to make your marriage a priority, so that when family pressure is brought to bear, and tension in the marriage is increased by these outside forces, you will know how to realign yourselves and make your marital integrity a priority.

Indulged Child and Caretaker

"Smothered with attention" was how Adam described his years at home surrounded by two maiden aunts and his devoted mother. His father ranked just below him in importance in the eyes of the three women. Everything from cutting his food to doing his laundry was magically handled by this ever-effective trio, who adored him and gave him the feeling that the world revolved around *him* rather than the sun. Well, at least *their* world did. But, like every young man who has to enter the world at large, Adam went to college and had the awakening of a lifetime. He learned that the people around him were not spending every waking hour thinking of what he was doing or what he was feeling. He learned that he could actually do things for himself, and took pride in his ability to cook some gourmet fare. He found that he could, with some effort, be generous to others—so long as he thought about it ahead of time! He amazed himself when he left dorm life and got an apartment so he could live on his own. He rather liked the solitude, the control he had over his daily life, the ability to do what he wanted without the benefit of overly concerned, clucking relatives to watch his every move. Adam was developing away from his role of Indulged Child into a person living with more realistic expectations in the world.

Jill arrived at this same midwestern college after literally ejecting herself from her family of origin. She was the eldest of six kids and was, by dint of personality and birth order, designated the role of the Caretaker. Her mother was very busy with civic affairs and was often disorganized when it came to home life and her children. Jill often picked up the slack and met the needs of the other five children with efficiency and love. When she left home, she traveled much the same road as Adam, for different reasons. She found the solitude of a single room delightful. She ate in the dining hall instead of cooking in her own suite. She went to parties but didn't host any. She made friends with highly competent independent students who didn't see her through the same Caretaker lens that her family had looked through. What a relief. She was enjoying herself, looking out for herself and caring *only* for herself.

One day in the library she was sitting at a table and a handsome fellow came to join her, introducing himself as Adam. Well, romance began. She loved his apartment, the food he cooked for her, the way he seemed so independent and able to take care of himself. She appealed to Adam for her ability to allow him to do his own thing without questioning; she was, after all, spending a lot of her energy on just taking care of her own needs and desires.

The marriage took place after graduation, and though Adam's aunts and mother wept at the wedding, he was happy. Despite the fact that Jill's mother was ill and the family had hoped she would delay her wedding to come home and take care of her, Jill did not relent. She married Adam with a happy heart. All was well.

Adam's work was very stressful, and he was exhausted every night when he came home. Jill's work at a local school got her home several hours before Adam. Jill took up doing the laundry and Adam stopped doing the cooking. But they managed to maintain a semblance of their newfound selves. Adam helped whenever Jill asked for it, and she was still finding time to take a watercolor course and participate in a fine literature club. He often retreated to the den to work while she washed dishes and straightened the house. They were happy, though, until Adam's aunts came to "inspect" the newlyweds' apartment and see their dearest Adam.

In subtle and not so subtle ways, the Aunts implied that Jill had fallen short of the mark when it came to taking care of their beloved nephew. They jokingly reported how the pie she had baked, though delicious, wasn't Adam's favorite. They noticed that there was no special reading light for his desk in the den, and they wondered how he could show up at work with wrinkles in his shirt. Jill knew intellectually that the aunts' comments were excessive. But in her heart, she began to wonder if she had failed in some way. Adam kissed his aunts good-bye at the door and with a sigh of relief came back into the apartment. He hugged his wife, and playfully (or was it?) began to chide her for all the imagined misdemeanors she had committed that evening.

Despite their best efforts to maintain their newfound selves, they found that their secret thoughts echoed attitudes of the past. The next night, Adam vaguely criticized Jill's domestic skills. Jill found herself annoyed and torn as she ran out the door to make it in time for her watercolor class—after sewing a button on Adam's shirt. Tension began to build, and two weeks after the aunts' visit, they found themselves irritated at and disappointed in each other. What to do?

Their look in the Marriage Mirror didn't take long. They saw almost immediately that the aunts' visit had reactivated their designated roles from their families of origin. Adam and his father had been the King and Prince of their household. Constant attention had meant love to him as a youngster, so he sometimes felt unloved by Jill.

Jill was also stuck. She felt that showing love meant taking care of a person's every need, but as she was struggling to find a piece of her life that she could call her own, she felt unsupported and guilty every time she did anything that put her desires first. She didn't want to be seen as self-involved like her mother, but she didn't want to feel that every time she left for class, or left Adam alone to fend for himself, she was guilty of something horrible. They discussed the gamut of feelings they were experiencing, such as guilt, lack of support, and a sense of being unloved. They had to sit down and decide what they wanted their marriage to be like, and dispel the belief that love, to be real, can only come packaged the way you got it at home as a child. They also needed to learn how to interact with Adam's aunts without falling victim to those women's implied assessments of how the marriage was shaping up. The first step was looking in the Marriage Mirror. As with Carol and Rick, the next step will be turning to Section Two and finding out specifically what skills can help them.

Trailblazer and the Faint of Heart

Karen was born with a heart problem requiring risky surgery when she was five years old. Though she recovered and was expected to live a full and active life, her childhood was punctuated by her mother and father's overwhelming concern for her welfare. Her parents often seemed to relive the experience of her illness with tremendous anguish and distress. Comments such as "Watch out!" and "Are you sure you can do that?" were commonplace and became an integral part of her personality. Calling Karen "faint of heart" would be close to the truth. Karen was protected and discouraged from anything that required physical "risk." This was a constant frustration to her, since she secretly thought herself capable of the things her friends and siblings were doing. However, the role that was so deeply imprinted in her made her a cautious, sometimes timid and deliberate person. Whenever she would try to break away from her parents' overly protective ways, their worry and distress would stop her. She couldn't endure it when she felt she was causing them more suffering. On top of it all was her parents' own cautionary marital style. They rarely went anywhere or got carried away by anything. Karen was beginning to become a true reflection of the two of them.

Victor was his family's "point man." He always tried new and daring activities. His parents relied on him to return home with tales of his feats and could appreciate them all the more because they had a sense of fun and expansiveness that enabled Victor to become the man he was. They admired his ability to try anything once and often joked with him that if he would do it first, they would do it later.

One could wonder what Karen and Victor might have in common that would even bring them into the same room. Faith, it seems. They met at a church function. Karen, with her resplendent red hair, attracted Victor immediately. Once they got to talking, Karen found herself fascinated by his adventuresome spirit and ability to be free. In fact, they were a perfect match. Each felt at home with the other. Victor found he had a familiar audience for his travel reports. Karen had spent a lifetime listening enthralled to the adventures of others, and Victor's reports were so exciting and compelling. He also saw someone who had a secret wish not just to listen but to participate. Victor tempted her with dreams of ventures they could do together. Karen comforted him with familiar encouragement and respect for his attitude toward life.

Engaged soon after they met, they prepared their honeymoon trip to Africa. Karen's sense of trepidation, so familiar to her, was eased by Victor's supreme confidence in their ability to have a safe, exciting, and wonderful experience together. For the first time Karen felt that she was going to realize all the possibilities of her life. All was well until Karen's parents caught wind of what they were planning. They phoned her in a state of complete distress. How could they think of such a trip? Karen's health would be threatened by dysentery, smallpox, even the rare but deadly Ebola virus. They forgot to mention lions and hyenas and elephants! All of a sudden, Karen began to doubt the wisdom of such a trip. Wouldn't Victor really rather see the Grand Canyon? He became furious, first at Karen, and then at her family for planting the seeds of doubt, when she had been so free and excited while planning the Africa trip.

Victor charged around his apartment as Karen listened to him describe what her parents were doing to her—how they were asking her to continue to make them feel comfortable, when she was in no danger and had a right to her own life. Articulated this way, it was a message that Karen understood clearly for the first time. She could not live out her role of the faint of heart to keep her parents from worrying. For the first time she found herself angry at their interference. What to do?

Through articulating his frustration with her parents' interference, Victor had given Karen a glimpse into the Marriage Mirror that enabled her to see clearly the ways in which her parents' needs had shaped her behavior and her role in her family. By "borrowing" Victor's anger at them, she was able to experience how stifling and demanding they had been. But how was she going to be able to go on the honeymoon without worrying about them worrying? She began to waffle daily about their honeymoon plans. They were in serious trouble. Victor knew that unless Karen made the break from her parents now, she would have even more difficulty later. Victor could not imagine his life stifled and controlled in that way. He knew he would have to consider breaking off the engagement. Karen also knew that she could not expect a man like Victor to live a life catering to a frightened wife.

The faith that had brought them together months before was called upon again as Karen made the most adventurous move of her life. She had to believe in the rightness of her decision to marry Victor. She had to believe in the rightness of joining her star to his. She had to have faith that her parents would not die from their distress, but would survive to see their daughter home in one piece at the end of the trip. By *borrowing* Victor's resolve, Karen took that leap of faith and found herself on safari in Africa, having the time of her life. Subsequent adventures that she and Victor took always met with a call of concern from her parents and a few niggling worries of her own, but soon Karen learned that she needn't carry her old role or her parents' fears into her marriage.

The tradition of giving silver or fine china as a wedding gift should be replaced by the giving of a mirror, beautiful, sturdy, and clear. It should be hung in a place of honor and prominence in every home the couple inhabits. They could consult it throughout their years together when they are in need of sorting out the confusing behaviors and conflicts that beset them as a couple. Sometimes all it takes is a quick glimpse to see the origins of a problem. Sometimes there will be no answers at all. But they will always have the opportunity to cast their own reflections anew—something they may have forgotten they have the right and capability to do. Whether they are Peacemakers or Rebels,

Trailblazers or among the faint of heart, the Marriage Mirror offers people a chance to modify the influence of their parents' marriages and the roles created for them in their own families.

Renegotiating Attachments

CHAPTER THREE

The Cast of Characters

You say, "I do," and suddenly you are the recipient of yet another set of parents. For better or worse, in sickness and in health, till death do you part, the six of you are about to journey through your life together. Marriage exponentially increases the number of people, expectations, and feelings you have to deal with on a daily basis. Even more staggering is the fact that if this is a second or third marriage for either one of you, and if you have children, there are upwards of six or eight additional "parent types" who entertain the idea that they should be a critical part of your married life. As an individual or part of a couple, you will have to interact with all these people. Couples often find themselves stunned by the impact of these new relationships on themselves and on their marriage. Even the briefest interaction with a parent or an in-law can raise the most powerful feelings. It could be a letter from Arizona where the folks have retired, a phone call from across town, or a simple overnight visit for the holidays. Couples find themselves awash on a sea of expectations from without as well as within.

The Mother-in-Law

The old joke goes like this. A parish priest went to see his parishioner to make arrangements for the funeral of the man's mother-in-law. He inquired solicitously: "And what was the complaint that was responsible for her passing?" To which the woman's son-in-law replied in bewilderment, "Complaint? There was no complaint. Everybody around here was quite satisfied."

Mother-in-law. Just the utterance of the word often brings fear into the hearts of even the most intrepid couple. But why does this mother-in-law have such a bad reputation? Why do jokes describing her as either dangerous or foolish abound in our culture? Where does all this real and imagined tension originate from? Dr. Evelyn Duvall, in her book *In-Laws Pro and Con*, discusses the origin of mother-in-law avoidance.[6]

This is a concept practiced all around the world. Among the northern tribes of Australia, if a man was found talking to his mother-in-law, he was reprimanded and banished from the camp. The Yucatan Indians believe that if a man meets his mother-in-law, he can never beget children. Among the Navahos here in America, mothers-in-law are never supposed to look upon their sons-in-law, and therefore are often not at the weddings of their daughters. In some tribes in Africa, mother-in-law avoidance is observed even after the death of a man's wife. As far back as 1922, Scottish anthropologist James G. Frazer was musing in his book, *The Golden Bough*, that "The awe and dread with which the untutored savage contemplates his mother-in-law are amongst the most familiar facts of anthropology."[7]

It has been suggested that the tension between mothers-in-law and sons-in-law originated in ancient cultures, where it was a protection against incest in the form of unconscious fantasy. It has also been suggested that mother-in-law avoidance was a form of "cutting" by which the mother-in-law rejects the son-in-law as an interloper and stranger. Whatever explanation one subscribes to, mother-in-law avoidance has a rightful place in folklore and history. It is therefore not surprising that it is a substantial issue in contemporary marriages as well. We find remains of it in our culture couched in terms of mother-in-law jokes, modern attitudes, and expectations. Mother-in-law tensions do not just arise between a man and his mother-in-law, but between a woman and her mother-in-law as well.

The most common criticisms of the mother-in-law, according to Dr. Duvall, is her need to actively intrude and interfere in the life of the married couple. She often acts as though the couple are still her children to criticize, discipline, and protect. These intrusions of course serve to blunt the couple's attempts at independence and keep them responding as children, thus justifying her position that they need her guidance.

You may recognize some of these complaints:

"She can't let go of her son."
"She buys her daughter more expensive gifts than I can afford."
"She always has her two cents to throw in about how we are raising the kids."
"She nags about how we manage our finances."
"I wish she wouldn't worry about us so much . . . she calls every day!"
"Why does she always have to tell us how lonely she is?"

When these and other issues arise, they are no joke to the couple who are trying to make their way through marriage. An offhand comment from a woman's mother-in-law as she passes by the kitchen door at a family gathering can throw the marriage into a tailspin. "Oh, I don't think Billy should eat those quiche hors d'oeuvres—his cholesterol is so high. Didn't he tell you?" It matters little that Billy and his wife have been working on his cholesterol level for two years. It matters only that his mother's offhand comment assumes that his wife is not doing her job of taking care of Billy. Later that evening when all the guests have gone home, Billy discovers he has a big problem with his wife that seems to him to be coming out of nowhere. Possibly she begins to rail against his mother . . . and how she will never measure up as a wife in her eyes. Possibly she is furious at Billy for letting his mother go on thinking that his cholesterol is high when she has been working to get it under control for the past two years by changing the food she prepares for him. It was a simple comment, made in passing, that shattered the day for Billy's wife and later for Billy. Meantime, his mother went home without realizing the havoc she had wrought! Or did she?

His mother was exercising her right as protective mother. This job is extremely difficult to give up. Anyone who has been a mother can tell you that. Indeed, Billy's mother may never be able to stop herself from commenting in this way, so it is up to the couple to find ways of anticipating her actions and curtailing her impact on their feelings for and interactions with each other.

The Father-in-Law

Oddly, it is almost impossible to find a father-in-law joke to place right here. Jokes often have at their core a component of hostility. Traditionally, in our culture, it has been easier to express hostility toward women than toward men, who are seen as authority figures. In any event, fathers-in-law have a special dynamic role they play with couples. They are not to be underestimated!

The most common complaints about fathers-in-law, according to Dr. Duvall, involve their tendency to want to dominate and interfere. Holding onto his position as family patriarch, the father-in-law may feel he has the right, knowledge, and experience to guide the married couple even when they no longer need his guidance. It keeps his position of "top banana" intact, and it enables him to delay the day when his power base is threatened by the next generation. Much of the behavior of fathers-in-law comes directly from loss or fear of loss of status.

You may recognize some of these complaints:

"He is unable to adjust his ideas to the changing times."
"He likes to dominate his family."
"He criticizes how we raise the kids, what we spend money on and how my wife makes the holiday meals."
"He doesn't seem interested in us or the kids . . . not in anything we do."

From the tenuous perch of patriarch, the father-in-law may hurl down comments that sting as well as undo a couple's conviction about the direction they have been taking on any given issue.

Faith and her husband, Larry, had gone out and purchased their first new car. Over the years they had had used cars, but they were finally in a position to buy one fresh off the assembly line. For them it was an emotional decision, and they bought the car based on physical appeal, what they called its "snazziness" factor. When Faith stopped by her elderly in-laws' house to bring over some groceries she had picked up for them (they were no longer able to drive themselves), she was greeted by her father-in-law with a *Consumer Reports* magazine in his hand. As she put the groceries away for them, she was treated to a harangue about how the car they chose wasn't top-rated, how Larry had never been that impulsive before. He went so far as to muse about the fact that it must have been Faith's idea to get the car. He said they had been impulsive and should have come by his house to look at the magazine before making such a big purchase. He ended by saying, "Mark my words, you're going to have trouble with that car." All this, mind you, from a man who could no longer drive his own car. Once she got home, Faith began to stew. She was annoyed with her father-in-law for taking the fun out of the car for her, but that soon transformed itself into annoyance with Larry. Why hadn't he checked *Consumer Reports*? Larry got home and found himself sideswiped by his wife's attack on him.

Faith's father-in-law was exercising his right as patriarch of the family. It was a position that was showing signs of fading. His own frailty and inability to be autonomous left him with very few of the trappings of his status as father, advisor, and family leader. She and Larry must learn to anticipate and modify his increasing attempts to flex his patriarchal muscles now that he is getting older. They must learn to recognize what he is doing, and refrain from taking it out on each other.

The Art of Anticipation

It is often helpful for couples to look at the type of parents they had when they were growing up to anticipate the type of parents and in-laws those people will make after they are married. People often make the mistake of thinking, "When I'm married, things will be different with my folks. They'll see that I'm finally independent and leave me alone." Or, later in the marriage, "Now that I have kids of my own, I will be on a more equal footing with my parents." Or even, "Now that we've moved my wife's mom and dad to a retirement village, we'll have more time to ourselves." Like leopards, parents rarely change their stylistic spots after their child marries. If couples can forcast how their parents or in-laws will interact with them, they can sometimes mitigate the power and impact that interaction will have on them as a couple.

Parents do not always act in complete concert with one another, and a couple may find that while the husband's mother is a hands-off type, his father may expect to maintain the chummy, overly involved relationship that he had with his son before his son got married. Some parents have such a unity of purpose and function that couples can predict their parents' behavior as if they were dealing with one person. No matter which of these two scenarios a couple faces, it is important for them to learn how to assess their parents' behavior. Following are a few examples that will jump-start your awareness of how the new cast of characters in your marriage can be understood and anticipated.

Contact-Hungry Parents and In-Laws

You know or have heard of parents or in-laws like these. They can never seem to get enough of their child and his or her spouse. They want to see them every holiday, every weekend, and, with the advent of grandchildren, feel completely entitled to daily reports of progress. They pose no threat to life and limb, and are in general loving and interested parents. It is only when their style of relating butts up against the expectations of one or both members of the couple that problems can arise.

"This daughter-in-law business is something I didn't bargain for," says Robin, a party planner who has been married to Phil for seven years. "My in-laws are very nice people, but they keep wanting me to be their *daughter*. In Phil's family, that means daily contact and no thoughts too personal to be private! My parents aren't like that and let us be. My in-laws call all the time and ask what we are doing, if we can get together, or even our opinion on the smallest thing. My husband doesn't always get on the phone for these conversations, leaving a lot of the talking to me. He thinks I should call his mom with news and chat all the time. I think he just wants to be off the hook with his folks after years of their calling to talk when he was single. Seems as if it's my job to manage his parents . . . and I don't like it!"

Robin has been dealing with her in-laws and Phil's expectations for seven years without any resolution of the problem. Every time Phil's mom mentions to him that she wishes she heard from *them* more often, Phil gets annoyed with Robin and they end up fighting. Phil feels that Robin is shirking her responsibility. She accuses him of putting everything on her shoulders and making her feel guilty for not being a good enough daughter-in-law. She feels that she has been dealing with them for seven years, and now it's Phil's turn to help out a little. She spends alot of time angry at Phil and caught between his wishes, her in-laws, and her own familiarity with how her own family handles contact. What to do?

The Marriage Mirror would be a good place for these two to begin their discussion. First, an appraising look at the differing ways their own parents handled contact with them as individuals would clue them in to the obviously differing expectations held by each set of parents. Phil's parents were contact-hungry, with a long line of contact-hungry relations to commend them. His grandparents had an almost peerlike relationship with his parents. They were more friends than parents and grown children. Robin's grandparents had attempted such boundary-leaping with poor results. Her parents and grandparents had always had a strained relationship. That is why Robin's parents were so scrupulous about giving Robin and Phil their space. They didn't want a replay of the tensions they had experienced as a young couple. Along the way, Robin might take note of the fact that her role in her family was that of a Peacemaker, and she naturally assumed that role with her husband and in-laws. Phil might acknowledge his role in his family as the "golden boy" who could do no wrong in the eyes of his parents, and whom they always saw as their greatest success. After all, his life gave them great joy.

In the course of discussion, Phil realized that he had often felt burdened by his role as golden boy. He often felt that his success was so much his parents' success that he could never fail them. Yes, he could admit that Robin's taking over most of the contact with his folks left him feeling freer than he ever had. However, this meant that she had to maintain the level of contact that would keep his parents comfortable, or Phil would become tense and consequently angry at Robin for failing him in some way. *Herein lay so much of the strain between Phil and Robin.* Once they gained a better understanding of where the pressure originated from, they were able to be a bit more sympathetic to each other, and some of their frustration and anger washed away. However, they are at a precarious point in the true resolution of their conflict. Now they must find a way of *anticipating* and *modifying* the effect his parents have on the two of them.

They knew they could count on the next phone call. They knew they could count on questions that sought to reveal every nuance of their daily lives. They knew they could count on Phil feeling the anxiety to meet his parents' need and Robin's wish to head for the hills! Oddly, their newfound understanding of what was happening between them made it possible for Robin to answer the ringing phone that evening with more serenity than she had in a while. Phil got on the extension, talked for a while, and then he hung up, leaving Robin to continue the conversation. He walked by her, and they exchanged a wink and a smile, attesting to their newfound understanding and respect for each other. Robin felt empowered to cut the conversation a bit shorter this time, and Phil found that he didn't have to struggle with quite so much guilt as he had in the past. This couple's understanding and anticipation of Phil's parents' behavior helped to go a long way in their ability to join together and find a solution. It also helped them to avoid the marital conflict that his parents' style often generated.

Undermining Parents and In-Laws

Richard, a physical therapist in private practice, reports:

"My father-in-law has never thought that I was good enough for his daughter. He doesn't understand our relationship. He belittles me often, usually in a joke, but most of the time you can't miss the message. My wife can't say a bad thing about her dad, and she just turns the other cheek and tells me I should too. Maybe I could, if I didn't feel that my wife partly believed her dad when he says those things about me."

Richard feels that his father-in-law deliberately makes these comments to drive a wedge between him and Beth. He was sure that his father-in-law wanted to keep Beth around to take care of him in his old age; at least that was his most recent theory. Beth was very attached to her father and had never really come to terms with the changes in allegiance that marriage naturally brings. She never realized how important it was for her to take a stand when her father made cutting jokes about her husband. She figured that if they simply ignored it, there would be no confrontation and eventually her father would tire of making them.

At a recent Thanksgiving dinner, Beth's dad pulled his usual stunt and made Richard the butt of a joke, though, as always, it was hard to tell if he meant it or not. If confronted, his father-in-law would deny any malevolent motive and use the opportunity to ridicule Richard for being too sensitive. Richard could barely bring himself to shake his father-in-law's hand upon leaving. While Beth threw her arms around her dad as always and expressed her love on parting, Richard was fuming.

On the way home, Beth found herself subtly picking at Richard for real and imagined faults. After being unable to express himself directly to his father-in-law all afternoon, and now being attacked by Beth, he turned his fury on her. He ranted and raved at her for not stopping her father's attacks. He felt that she had the power to do so, and she would not come to his defense. Normally glib and able to wield words when he needed to, Richard was unable to find any. Beth's silence with her father on the matter was deafening as far as he was concerned, and he felt that he could not go on in a marriage when he half suspected his wife of sharing her father's disapproving feelings toward him. "Why did you marry me, anyway?" he asked at the end of the argument. What to do?

Maybe that is a good place for them to start. Why did they marry each other, anyway? Often when a couple actually reviews the reasons for their attraction and eventual marriage, they are able to recall and reexperience a wealth of feelings that anger and disappointment have sealed over. Opening a discussion there—especially when the question has just been actually asked by one or both of the spouses— is a good thing to do.

Then, Richard and Beth needed to take the requisite look into the Marriage Mirror. Richard came from a household in which he had little or no respect for his father, and so his father's disparaging remarks and barbs were eased by his knowledge that they came from an uninformed mind. His mother was a passive woman who didn't stand up for the children, let alone for herself. He had always been a bit embarrassed about his family, and was highly critical of them himself. In the case of Beth's dad, however, he actually respected the man as intelligent and clear-thinking (at least when it came to anything not having to do with him).

Beth came from the devoted arms of her parents directly to Richard. Her father was her idol, and her mother supported that view at every turn. In their household, nobody else was as good, as smart, or as special as they were. They lived under a kind of collective delusion with Beth's dad spearheading the fantasy. He was also the person who doled out the criticism about other people. Her dad's opinion meant a great deal to her—both what he thought of her and what he thought of Richard. She was used to seeing her mother back her father up all the time, but she had no idea that she was supposed to do that same thing for her own husband. She was still aligned with her dad. But don't mistake her; she loved her husband very much.

First they had to come to an understanding about what the problem was between them. Richard stated that he wanted her to support him the way he saw Beth's mom support Beth's dad. He wanted her to speak up on his behalf. When he verbalized that, he realized that he was asking her to do something for him that his own mother had never done.

Beth said that the only thing she was sure of was wanting him to gain the respect of her father so that she could be comfortable at these gatherings and not be torn between her father and her husband. When he asked her if she had respect for him, she was able to say that it was only at family gatherings that she experienced any doubts about him. The long arm of her father's criticism at least didn't extend all the way to their house!

Each of them wanted the *other* to make it "right" for them. But in the end, it was up to both of them to change the events that brought pressure to bear on them. Richard had to begin to speak up for himself. He needed to realize that expecting his wife to speak up for him was only giving his father-in-law more ammunition. Beth needed to look at the issue of her allegiance and learn to live with a bit of discomfort in order to support Richard's efforts to get what was due him. Both Richard and Beth need to read the next three chapters to help them make the alignment adjustments necessary to stay on track with each other. Once they have decided on a plan of action, they need to anticipate Beth's father's behavior and their own, in order to create a new ending to their usual dinner table scene.

Martyred vs. Dictatorial Parents and In-Laws

Wendy and David's situation illustrates how two sets of parents with opposite styles of interacting can nearly paralyze a marriage. David's parents' style can best be characterized as dictatorial. They would do anything they could to get what they wanted from the couple. They bullied, intimidated, and cajoled if they wanted to see the grandkids or take them out for dinner. Their demands were not always excessive; they were just entirely without regard for Wendy and David's needs. At the other extreme, Wendy's parents played martyr. They were experts at heaving a sigh of disappointment when Wendy and David couldn't get together with them, but they never insisted. They carried around with them a kind of victimized quality. They always gave in at those times when David's parents and they were "scrambling" to see who would get to be with the kids. Their most powerful weapon was guilt, and it was most evident when it reflected off the glare of David's parents' selfish dictatorship.

Wendy and David met each holiday with trepidation. The tension between them would begin months in advance. David's folks would begin with a litany of reasons why they needed to see them. Wendy's parents would stake a claim but back away at the least sign of conflict. The parents never actually had a fight with each other over this, because Wendy's parents were so good at acquiescing. It was Wendy and David who argued over the arrangements. It was always the same. David defended his parents not so much because he thought they were right, but because he knew in his heart it was futile to fight. Wendy felt the need to battle for her parents when they couldn't do it themselves. What to do?

Quick, consult the Marriage Mirror!

Wendy had spent a lifetime with ineffectual parents. She saw how they allowed themselves to be taken advantage of or treated poorly. The only way they could get what they wanted was through making those around them feel so guilty that they would yield to their wishes. She had learned at their knee that she did not want to be that way and so had educated herself to fight for her rights. Once married, she had found herself angry at them for being unable to stand up for themselves. She was angry at David's parents for always being so overpowering. She was angry at David for never championing her parents' side. Their arguments were always the same.

David had spent a lifetime with parents who always ended up getting what they wanted. They achieved this by wearing away people's resistance until finally they could do nothing but give in to pressure. They really weren't bad people, and were always generous to their children, but they simply had no idea how their enthusiasm and persistence in getting their own way was affecting those they loved. David had learned to sidestep the struggle with his parents by recognizing the inevitability of their "winning." He didn't fight them. Moving out as a young adult hadn't done much to temper their insistence and power over him, but he had thought that once he got married that would change. No such luck. He often used Wendy's anger to propel him forward and take a stand, but he could rarely do this without first having a fight with her that would empower him.

In every marriage there is true power, which, when exercised properly, can bring the couple closer, afford them more ease in handling parental pressure, and set appropriate boundaries for the families involved. David had given up this power by using futility and hopelessness as his excuse. Wendy had also missed her opportunity for true power because her anger always got in her way, either in her interaction with David or with her parents. Wendy and David were suffering because all the power of their marriage was in the hands of their parents. They had never taken the opportunity to realign themselves and recognize the authority they had as adults and as a couple. They were unwilling to face the discomfort and the hard work involved in taking the power of their marriage back and guiding the influence their parents' styles was having on them.

It doesn't matter whether you identify your parents as dictatorial, or martyred, contact-hungry or undermining—or if you give them another appellation altogether. It matters only that you and your spouse take the time to describe them, identify them, and anticipate their actions. By doing this, you will create a private well of understanding between you that strengthens your relationship yet affords you an avenue for compassion toward your parents. This exercise paves the way to modifying their influence and maximizing your enjoyment of them.

CHAPTER FOUR

The "Royal We" of Marriage

"Peace, commerce, and honest friendship with all nations; entangling alliances with none."
Thomas Jefferson[8]

For centuries, kings and queens have invoked the blessing of the gods to empower them as monarchs. As far back as A.D. 1230, Louis IX of France was called *Saint* Louis for his pious crusades and believed closeness to God. And, of course, we've all heard of the famous quote of Queen Victoria of England when she saw a groomsman mimicking her. "*We* are not amused," she said with all the hauteur she could muster. She didn't say, "*I* am not amused." So what is this "We" business?

To empower themselves, to validate their decisions, to appear holy and deserving, kings and queens spoke of themselves as being one with God; hence the "Royal We" when describing their actions or thoughts. Subjects were to regard them with something amounting to the same awe with which they regarded God. In the case of Queen Victoria, how much more effective a message of displeasure did she convey when she implied through the "We" that not only she, but God Himself, was vexed by the groomsman's impertinence?

Monarchy in days of yore was often absolute. That meant that everything from fashion to foreign policy was dictated by the king or queen. Few deigned to question the decisions of the king, lest his head be found bobbing on the end of a gatepost in a public square. The power that the king or queen had to control his or her own life and the lives of others was increased by the general acceptance by their subjects that God was in on it too.

When a marriage took place between monarchies, forces of allegiance and power were brought together to make one yet more mighty realm. This is the reason that royal marriages were based on territory or trade, never on love. And though any king who sent his daughter abroad to marry a foreign prince in order to secure peace, power, or trade didn't expect her to *love* her new husband, he did expect her to vow her *allegiance* to him. It was often the case that the young girl never saw her family again once she was sent abroad to marry. It was thought that even the sight of her old family might endanger her allegiance to her new liege and country.

One might look upon this rule that separated young girls from their families as discriminatory. But this rule transcended gender; even princes were required to bind their allegiance to their new country. Queen Victoria's husband Prince Albert was born in Coburg, Germany, and upon his marriage, he had to renounce his allegiance to his native country. He spent his lifetime (brief though it was) working on behalf of the British people. But like many in-laws, the British people *always* saw Albert as a meddling foreigner, an interloper.

The concept of the "Royal We" and the clear definition of *allegiance* works as well in the marriages of private citizens with no claim to the throne at all. It even works in marriages that thrive in democracies! It's just that not many people know of the power of the "Royal We," and fewer still make sure to clarify their allegiances after marriage.

Pledging Allegiance

"It is not the oath that makes us believe the man,
but the man the oath."
Aeschylus[9]

A pledge of allegiance made by one royal family to another was clear-cut. Once the pledge was made, boundaries would not be breached, and a whole system of etiquette supported and protected the allegiance. The way modern marriage approaches the concept of allegiance is more difficult for couples. It requires more balancing, since two powerful family forces are vying for their fealty and attention. The expectations of loyalty that emanate from a person's family are as powerful as the strongest electromagnetic field. Some families have highly exacting rules for meeting their requirements for loyalty and allegiance. Sometimes the pull is so strong that a man or woman must borrow the strength of his or her spouse to keep from being pulled away from the marriage back into the magnetic embrace of their family. And sometimes, a person can't resist the pull at all.

Still other families require no specific displays of loyalty and allegiance, but leave it up to the married child to find a way of demonstrating those qualities. These families do not give up their claims, they are usually just less noisy about them.

Some families actually work to undermine budding allegiances in the marriage by splitting the couple through the device of blaming the in-law child for all they are unhappy with, and preserving their view that their child remains pledged to them.

In yet other families, even deceased parents can stake their claim to allegiance. An imprint of a parent's expectation is left even after he or she is long gone. It is common to show loyalty to a memory by behaving in ways that would have been approved of by the deceased. Conflict can easily arise as one spouse clearly feels he or she is "fighting a ghost."

High-Voltage Parents

Robin and Phil of Chapter Three came up against two very thorny issues with regard to allegiance. First, their families had very different requirements when it came to demonstrating allegiance and loyalty. Robin's family had a low-voltage set of expectations. They seemed to function with the faith that Robin and Phil would be available to them at times and come to them if they needed to. Phil's folks were highly demanding of Phil and Robin's time, opinions, and information. They had high-voltage expectations when it came to allegiance and loyalty. Second, the ways that Phil and Robin had incorporated their parents' differing expectations of allegiance into their marriage was beginning to cause friction and sparks between them.

Robin no longer wanted to meet the requirements set down by Phil's parents. She no longer wanted to be the one to intercede so that Phil wouldn't get sucked back in with them. She wanted Phil to be strong enough to resist the magnetism of their expectations.

The conventional wisdom is that wedding vows are tantamount to pledges of allegiance, and that with marriage the valence of a child's loyalties shifts automatically to his or her spouse. Parents are supposed to step gracefully aside into second place. If they refuse to accept the new order, they invariably cause problems. This, in fact, was what Phil's parents were doing. However, the onus cannot be completely upon them. They hadn't gotten with the program and stepped aside—and they exacted much in the way of filial allegiance. Nevertheless, Phil and Robin had made their wedding vows filled with expressions of loyalty, but the way in which they had handled the situation over so many years proved that words alone cannot enforce a pledge.

Phil had never clearly declared his complete allegiance to Robin. He showed this by the way he put pressure upon her to meet the demands of his parents without regard to the way it made her feel. He also paid no attention to the message it was sending to his folks about what they could expect from them as a couple. Robin, for her part, had gone along with it by allowing herself to play the role of devoted daughter-in-law and meet their filial requirements. She also had not addressed the pangs she often felt about how little time this left her for her own folks.

This is not an uncommon problem for young couples. The skill it takes to actually recognize the magnetic pull of each set of parents is often hard-won. Some couples never learn it and find themselves a lifetime later still trying to meet these demands while ignoring the effect it has on their marriage or on themselves personally.

Elaine, a 62-year-old housewife and part-time office worker, found herself in that situation after 32 years of marriage:

> "My in-laws are now in their eighties and living on their own . . . thank God! They have always demanded a lot of our time. My husband is their only son, and we don't live that far from them. My husband has always felt a strong obligation to them. They had moved to the United States from Italy to get him the education and prospects he deserved. I guess he has always felt he needed to pay them back for the sacrifice. We were informed early on in our marriage that they expected to spend Christmas, Easter, and New Year's with us. Foolish children that we were, we complied, and my family ended up with birthdays and lesser holidays to look forward to seeing us. My folks weren't very demanding, and I guess they felt that rather than fight it, they would find alternatives to

being with us. I wasn't aware of very much back then except wanting to please my in-laws and be accepted. I also didn't want any conflict with my husband, who didn't seem to notice that *we* never got to choose what we would be doing for the holidays. I never thought a pattern set back in the early days of my marriage would last for 32 years!

The other day something happened that opened my eyes to what I had been doing all this time. My own daughter is recently married to a lovely boy, and as Christmas approached I began to talk to her and her husband about them coming with us to Grandma and Grandpa's house. I naturally thought they would want to be with us. I spoke without thinking and was caught short when my son-in-law, after casting a quick glance at my daughter, who nodded, suddenly interrupted me and said, "We'll have to get back to you, Mom. Sara and I haven't decided how we are going to divide up the holidays this year." Well! Of course I was stunned and pretty upset. I was even a little angry. But after they had left, I realized how envious I was of them. How did they do that so effortlessly? It's something that in 32 years of marriage I had never been able to say to my in-laws."

When a couple makes efforts early on to establish their primary allegiance to each other, they are often met with their parents' shock, anger, and emotional upset, especially if the parents are of the high-voltage variety. The process is a difficult one. However, in this case, Elaine only needed to be given the message once. When the next set of holidays came around, Elaine called and asked what their plans were. She still expressed her wish for them to be with her and her husband, but she no longer simply expected her daughter and son-in-law's allegiance to rest in her house. She had respect, tempered with a bit of envy, for their willingness to act as one.

Low-Voltage Parents

Who fights for the rights of the low-voltage parents and in-laws? They tend to be the type of parents who find it difficult to ask for what they want from the couple. They often lose out to higher-voltage parents when it comes to family time together. They don't have enough of a magnetic field around them to "pull in" the attention they may wish for. What often happens is that their own child has to fight for their rights within the context of his or her marriage. Remember Robin's pangs about not spending enough time with her folks because Phil's parents were so high-voltage and demanding? For quite some time Robin did nothing to insist that her parents be given equal time. However, once she got in touch with the fact that she no longer was willing to constantly bow to the pressure that Phil's parents brought to bear upon them, she also got in touch with the injustice in her own parents being given such short shrift. Soon, she found herself fighting for their long-neglected rights to a piece of the loyalty pie. New tension arose between Phil and Robin, because she had never before insisted on dividing their time more equally. This threw Phil into a state of anxiety, as he knew his parents would increase the voltage and try to reestablish their supremacy. He knew how tense this would make him feel. Phil's true pledge of allegiance to his wife meant meeting her needs as well when it came to her family.

Couples who have a mix of high- and low-voltage parents will more often find themselves fighting internally than if they shared two sets of high-voltage parents. When that happens, a couple can often unite against the incredible pressure brought to bear on them. When a couple has two low-voltage sets of parents, they have a much easier time of it. It is important for couples to identify whether they have a high- or low-voltage set of parents. This helps them to anticipate problems ahead of time, but also enables them to recognize why they may be arguing so much between themselves. You may be saying that within your family, your mother is the high-voltage person and your father is low-voltage and really doesn't mind one way or the other what you do. Beware. It is often the case that the parent who is speaking the loudest is actually speaking for both. The quieter person gets to ride on the other one's coattails and reap the benefit of additional time with you, but never has to appear to be a demanding, difficult parent.

The most important thing to note, however, is that no matter the magnetic pull from parents, allegiance must reside within the couple. And a pledge of allegiance is only as sacred as the actions of the two partners taking that pledge.

Splitting and Blaming Parents

Another often severe problem that arises at these times of realignment is that a spouse's parents will blame the in-law child for being the force behind the decisions and new allegiances.

Scott, a 38-year-old systems analyst, confirmed this problem:

"My dad is a very demanding person, with high standards for achievement and excellence. That's okay, because I am too. When I married Barb, he was pretty clear that he didn't see her as smart enough, cultured enough, or social enough. Though he never said it, I always felt that he thought I had not made a good match. Of course, quite the opposite is true. Barb is a fantastic children's librarian and writes children's books, she's a devoted mother and wife, and we have lots of great time together. When an opportunity arose within my company to move to Chicago for a job with more prestige but not much more pay, Barb and I discussed it at length. Ultimately we decided that we would stay put and hope that the next opening would be more money and closer to home. We had the kids in a school that we liked, Barb loved where she was working, we had neighbors that meant a lot to us and, frankly, it felt as if we would be moving for the prestige rather than anything else. It didn't seem like a good enough reason to either of us. When my dad got wind of our decision, his immediate reaction was, 'Your wife can get a job anywhere but you have to be careful about advancing your career . . . can't Barb see that?' His immediate assumption was that Barb had unduly influenced me, implying that she wouldn't be looking out for me and my career and just wanted selfishly to hold me back. It's so typical. Whenever I do anything my father doesn't agree with, he blames it on Barb."

Scott's father doesn't get the message, and no matter how often Scott defends Barb or lets his father know that these are joint decisions that come out of a *true allegiance* to the well-being of the marriage, he continues to blame her. For her part, Barb was pretty fed up and angry. She frankly didn't understand why Scott continued to have so much contact with his dad. There were times when Barb and Scott would fight despite the fact that in principle, Scott agreed with her. But he loved his dad, and didn't know what to do. The question that each couple must ask themselves is whether or not they are behaving in a way that expresses their pledge of allegiance. By anticipating Scott's dad's blaming behavior, they had an opportunity to short-circuit it. They didn't have to tell him of the possibility of the promotion. This way they weren't leaving themselves open to the inevitable blaming of Barb that would follow. Additionally, a couple can use the certainty of the harangue to develop a sense of humor. Playful dialogues concocted between Barb and Scott anticipating his father's language and point of view broke the cycle of their frustration with each other.

Scott's dad is what you might call an intractable or obstinate parent. Dealing with such a person takes a great deal of patience and a strong will. Couples faced with this type of parent must work even harder to be clear about their pledge of allegiance to each other. For them, the private knowledge that they are pledged may be all they can hope for. Their parents may never understand or see the truth and value in that pledge.

Gone But Not Forgotten

Finally, it should be noted that people can maintain their filial allegiance to parents who are long gone. This can result in even more subtle difficulties than a couple might realize. Martha, a 40ish woman who lost her mother just a few years ago, tells it this way:

> "When I was growing up, my mother believed that it was important for us to dress a certain way when we went to school. This caused a lot of conflict because it was about that time that children were allowed to start wearing blue jeans to school. That didn't wash with my mother. She insisted on chinos for my brother and dresses or skirts for me. We were pretty mortified, and no amount of arguing seemed to make a dent. All I can tell you is that when I left home, I had a pair of blue jeans that were so worn, with so many patches on them that you could hardly find the original denim. I always wore them to her house and they drove her crazy! It was the '70s, you know. Well, now my girls are 12 and 14 and they want to dress like everyone else too, but the kind of clothes that girls are wearing now to school are more provocative, not to mention expensive. My husband knows that the girls want to fit in and he doesn't mind some of the clothing. We fight over it, and the other day I found myself shouting the words 'That's not the way we do it in *my* family!!' Those words hung in the air as my husband stared at me and said, 'I thought *we* were your family.' I hadn't realized what I had said."

Under stress and in the heat of the argument, Martha made a slip that unconsciously revealed how strong allegiance to one's original family can be. *"That's not the way we do it in my family"* implies that she still belongs to her original family and hasn't moved forward and formed her allegiance to her new family. This of course is not really the case on a day-to-day basis, but since the death of her mother, Martha has been feeling the unconscious pull of her old allegiances. As is often the case when a parent dies, the most efficient way of keeping him or her alive for you is to take on some of his or her characteristics and opinions. This is called introjection. You identify with the lost person completely and thus still have him or her with you. At these times, even a person who has already separated from parents and pledged a new allegiance can find himself or herself slipping back through time.

It takes effort and awareness to pledge allegiance to each other and make sure that the strong forces that families bring to bear upon you are moderated. For some couples, the fear of losing their parents' approval or invoking their anger keeps them from pledging allegiance to each other. Still others don't realize that they have options, rights, and the power to make this pledge and stick to it. The power of a marital union, like the power of a royal union, resides in the steadfastness and dependability of the pledge of allegiance made by its leaders. Royals not only believed that they could demand and receive these pledges of allegiance from their spouses, they also believed firmly in their right to control the forces from outside that might threaten their sovereignty. They invoked the "Royal We" whenever necessary and relied on it as a potent tool of their power. Couples have the same power residing in their marriages—they just need to know where to find it.

The "Royal We"

Using the concept of the "Royal We" involves more than just saying the word "we" when you and your spouse speak to your parents and want to appear as one. It is first and foremost a way of *thinking* about your marriage and *acting* in your marriage. It means accepting and embracing the rights you have as rulers of your own kingdom to define yourselves as you wish, to put the well-being of your people ahead of all others, and to protect the borders of your domain. One of its linchpins is the ability to *pledge allegiance* to your spouse. From there, defining together exactly where your *borders* will lie is essential. Finally, knowing how to *convey this information* (or issue royal decrees) in such a manner that neighboring kingdoms do not take up arms against you is a skill necessary to maintain a peaceable kingdom both from without and within.

Drake, a 36-year-old resident in cardiology, reported:

"We live in a small apartment building owned by my parents. Basically they're our landlords. Lately we find that my mom is using her pass key to come in unexpectedly. She always has what seems to be a good reason . . . measuring for the new dishwasher or checking on a possible leak to the apartment below us. This hasn't been too much of a problem in the past because my wife and I were never home. But six months ago we had a baby, and now Alice is home and starting to complain to me about how often my mom just POPS IN! She's afraid to say anything and, quite frankly, I'm not home much with my hours at the hospital and it doesn't affect me. I don't want my mom to think that she can't see the baby. Anyway, it seems a small price to pay. They give us a break on the rent and do a lot of little things for us."

Drake felt powerless to change the situation and expressed this by saying, "I feel like I'm between a rock and a hard place." Clearly Alice didn't appreciate being likened to either a rock or a hard place; she felt that his mother should be more sensitive and he should be stronger about their needs.

Drake said he would talk to his folks but put it off and never seemed to find the time. Alice, already tired from sleepless nights with the baby, was irritable and felt that his unwillingness to talk to his folks meant he didn't care about *her*.

Drake and Alice's problem is not uncommon. There has been a breakdown of the "Royal We" in their household. A few questions have to be asked to determine how the couple should proceed. Will Drake and his wife be able to uphold the pledge of allegiance they made years before to their marriage? Do they have any rights to define the borders of their kingdom, since they live in an apartment building owned by Drake's folks, who also appear to be quite generous to them? What are their worst fears about what will happen if they take some kind of stand on this issue? And finally, how do they convey the information to Drake's parents once they figure all this out? Let's discuss these fears one at a time.

Renewing the Pledge of Allegiance

Drake and Alice are a good team. They have fun together and respect each other. Their pledge had always been that they came first with each other. Before the baby, the strength of their pledge hadn't been tested. Their busy work lives left little time or choices when it came to seeing his or her parents, and that was accepted by everyone. But once the baby came and Alice was home all day, their pledge was sorely tested. Suddenly what had seemed so clear was confused. It was a shock to them both that they weren't really "together" or strong about the pledge they had made.

Reasserting your allegiance sometimes is necessary when situations change. The birth of their baby brought an enormous shift in the landscape of their lives. Everyone, including both sets of parents, was suddenly on new ground with them, and immediately the hands-off attitude everyone had taken before was no longer being heeded. Drake and Alice needed to take a moment to reexamine their allegiances. Their newest one was toward the baby. What was right for her was in the forefront of their decision-making. But it was hard for them to stick to this, because their parents naturally wanted to redefine allegiances once the baby was born. First Drake and Alice needed to think clearly about what their own pledge of allegiance consisted of; then and only then could they take into account the needs of the new grandparents.

Royal Rights to Boundaries

The question is whether Drake and Alice have boundary rights even though their personal kingdom lies within the walls of another's realm. Realistically this is a tough issue, but not for the reasons that may seem obvious. They certainly do have rights even though Drake's parents own the building. The rights that couples have are simple and can be most easily understood through referring back to the metaphor of the kingdom circumscribed by national boundaries.

Drake and Alice and the baby comprise a kingdom unto themselves, with laws that bind them and protect them. They design their own laws often without realizing that is what they are doing, and are constantly making amendments to them as their married life continues. For example, with the arrival of the baby, a new law was enacted in their kingdom requiring Drake to get home as soon as possible at the end of the day to relieve Alice and see the baby. Previous laws made allowances for Drake to go for coffee with the other residents at the end of a long day, or to spend long hours at the medical library just to "catch up on some ideas."

Laws also make reference to how and when foreigners may cross their borders. Till the birth of their little princess, there had been no attempts by foreigners to storm the borders. Now they needed to set up checkpoints and issue diplomatic invitations to visiting dignitaries from other realms in order to keep their borders intact and stay focused on their own subjects. Like any couple experiencing a lot of border crossings, they need to look in the Marriage Mirror first to determine how their family's marriages handled such things. From examining the past, they will get clues to their own behavior. Then they must determine exactly what types of borders they need in order to feel comfortable in their own home with their new baby. Then they must learn to feel comfortable issuing royal decrees.

Issuing Royal Decrees

This is the hard part. Privately couples may bolster themselves with "royal talk" and believe that they have rights and power, but when face to face with their parents (people who had previously held their child's allegiance in the palms of their hands), their resolve is often undone. They fear that they will become enemies of the other nearby kingdoms (parents, siblings, aunts and uncles). They fear that their "arrogance" in thinking that they have the right to demand respect as a separate kingdom will ultimately bring clashes and potential ruin to them. It is often more comfortable for couples at this point to open their borders to any and all comers. No matter the strain on their resources. No matter that they are losing control of their boundaries. No matter that their laws now count for nothing. Avoidance of border skirmishes with parents is the primary reason that couples refuse to use their power and issue royal decrees.

When Drake and Alice sat down to think about it, they realized their worst fear was getting Drake's folks so angry that they would think them ungrateful, would blame much of the shift in the rules on Alice and paint her as the bad one, and ultimately they would feel so uncomfortable that they would have to move our of their little haven. It might be added here that their fears were not groundless. Drake's mom was one to be generous, but she exacted a certain kind of guilty payback for her generosity. Drake's dad was quieter, but Drake had realized years ago that his father's silence often meant he agreed with what Drake's mother was doing.

A fear of angering one or both sets of parents is another

reason that couples don't attempt to utilize the "Royal We" and don't issue decrees more effectively. More often than not, couples are concerned about falling from grace, being cut off, and losing love. They'd rather keep everyone happy at great expense to themselves. Another reason is that couples fear hurting their parents and causing them distress. This is often seen with parents who seem to live through their children, thus making separation of any kind painful and disappointing for the parents. Yet one more factor that makes the assertion of rights so difficult is that couples actually want and often crave contact with their parents, but because they take no control of these contacts, they end up being frustrated.

In certain circumstances parents are to blame for either disrespecting a union or demanding too much filial allegiance after marriage. However, if couples try to clarify where their allegiance will lie, fix boundaries, issue clear royal decrees, and, in general, utilize the "Royal We," their parents will, more often than not, live by the laws of the land. If a couple does not take the time and effort to define these areas, they can be guaranteed that their parents will try to take control and determine these things themselves.

So how is it possible to present your decrees in a way that will be diplomatic, firm, and clear all at the same time? Chapter Six, "A Judicious Use of Power," will give specific instructions for how to speak up, how to be diplomatic, and how to enhance and preserve relations with parents while maintaining boundaries and exercising the "Royal We" of your marriage.

Counting on the Adaptability of Parents

Caught in their own fears of causing anger or distress in their parents by enforcing the "Royal We," a couple can lose sight of the fact that their parents have concerns of their own. Parents fear more than anything else the permanent loss of a child. It may be that they seem intractable and stubborn and you think, "What's the use of even trying?" Though it may seem that fighting the battle for sovereignty over your marriage is impossible, you may be surprised at just how pliable and adaptable they will be.

When a child marries, parents face a supreme adjustment in their thinking and approach to their own child. Most parents and in-laws know in their hearts that they can't go on treating their child the way they did when he or she was solely "theirs." However, they instinctively try to continue interacting in the old manner because, first and foremost, that is what they *know*. Just as a child must learn new ways of approaching his or her parents as a couple, so must parents learn new ways of speaking to and interacting with their child in the context of his or her new allegiance. One thing children can count on is the fact that their parents would rather do just about anything than lose them. Because of this deep resolve, parents are much more adaptable than couples realize. Chapter Six will offer some clear methods to begin testing this idea, giving you ways to speak with your parents that will enable them to adapt while still feeling cared about and wanted.

Every couple must realize that the wish and need for sovereignty and power over their own marriage is not a betrayal of their parents. It is rather a response to the natural order of nature and of society. Power, however, can be wielded in two ways. It can be absolute and show no flexibility, or it can be accessible and adapt when necessary. Couples should strive for the latter. Clearly, this type of power is easier to obtain when the couple has definitively pledged their allegiance to each other and when they are truly united in pursuit of the "Royal We." Once this is achieved, they can become flexible, generous sovereigns, because being so does not shake the foundation of their power or their ultimate rule.

CHAPTER FIVE

Coming to Consensus

*"We must all hang together, or assuredly we shall
all hang separately."*
Benjamin Franklin[10]

E veryone who is married has played this scene at least a
hundred times: You're ranting and raving about your
mother or father's latest infraction. Your spouse joins in to
echo your sentiments and agree with you, so naturally, you
attack your spouse as quickly as a lion attacks fresh meat.
They're not allowed to say such things about your parents.
Soon, you find yourself defending your folks, putting a new
slant on their behavior, casting a rose-colored light their
way. How in the world did you get to this place? Why suddenly are you taking sides with the very people who are making your life so difficult?

Though there are many answers to that question, the primary answer can be found once again in the issue of allegiance and the issue of trust. Is it truly possible to cast your
lot with your spouse, and not let guilty feelings drive you
backward into a position of aligned child instead of united
spouse? Is it possible to trust your spouse with your feelings,

both negative and positive, about your parents? Can you be sure that he or she will not misread your willingness to speak about your parents realistically as license to attack them at will? Is there hope that your spouse will acknowledge that facing the good and bad in your parents is not easy and should be handled with respect and support? Fortunately, the answer to all these questions is yes.

Consensus-Building

When working toward building consensus, each spouse is called upon to be as compassionate, patient, and nondefensive as possible. Understanding your parents' behavior and motivation toward you as a couple and as individuals is no small task. You might think that with all the complaining we do about our parents or in-laws, this would be a cinch. Even in our sleep most of us can rattle off lists of offenses perpetrated upon us by our parents. But the act of bringing these personal musings into the open air of critical discussion and consensus-building is another story entirely. Suddenly we are asked to join with our spouse to see our parents in the stark light of day. We are not only asked to do this, but to make determinations with our spouse cataloguing exactly which of our parents' qualities we can live with as a couple, and which ones instigate a marital call to arms. Those traits that we might have tolerated as individuals in our interactions with our parents may not be acceptable when we review them as a couple.

Working toward consensus enables a couple to have, as much as possible, a single view of their parents and the effect that their parents are having upon them as a couple. It is also important that they decide together where the limits of their endurance are with respect to their parents' behavior and operate from a unified position. From this position, if the need arises, they can set limits or confront a situation.

The following might be a typical dialogue that demonstrates a couple's need to work toward the beginnings of consensus:

SUSAN (*after getting off the phone with her mother*): "Why does she always have to arrange everything so far in advance? Now she's asking me what we are doing with the kids over Thanksgiving. It's months away! I can't plan next week! What does she want from me—a commitment that we'll be with her?"

GEORGE (*half listening to this familiar tirade*): "You know your mother. She tries to control all of her kids, and you're no exception."

SUSAN: "What do you mean?"

GEORGE (*thinking he is supporting Susan, but really joining in the attack*): "Come on, Susan. She's impossible. She has to know months in advance about Thanksgiving so she can make sure we don't make other plans and she can have the holiday the way she wants it. She's like that about everything. When have you ever been able to 'let her know' at *our* convenience?"

SUSAN (*beginning to shift position and defend her mother*): "Well, she has to be able to make plans. Since Dad died, she doesn't want to spend time alone and she naturally wants to know her plans ahead of time."

GEORGE: "You're dreaming. She's always been like this, even when your father was alive."

Susan and George have had this "conversation" a thousand times before. Susan always moves from being annoyed with her mother to defending the "poor woman's" motives and situation. The couple gets nowhere. George feels that he starts out supporting Susan and, for some crazy reason that he can't divine, ends up fighting with her.

Here's the same dialogue all over again, except this couple is working on building consensus in their marriage:

SUSAN: "My mom is impossible. She wants to know what our plans are for Thanksgiving. Why does she always want to know so far in advance what we are doing? I can't plan that far in advance. What does she want from us?"

GEORGE: "Look, Susan. You are getting yourself all worked up, and we both know that this happens all the time with your mom."

SUSAN (*instantly feeling protective of her mom*): "What do you mean?"

GEORGE: "This is your mom. We're not going to be able to change her. But I hate to see you so upset every time this happens. I have to admit that it annoys me, too. My only question is, what can we do about it?"

SUSAN: "Well, she's alone and misses my dad. She naturally wants to know what her plans are going to be. She's not young anymore, you know."

GEORGE (*not making his usual attack here*): "I understand that. I sympathize with her, but maybe you and I need to decide just what we can do so it doesn't get us caught up short every time." (*George is gently suggesting using the art of anticipation.*)

SUSAN (*feeling less defensive*): "We really should. I guess we can't change her. What should we do?"

This couple is now on the road to coming to consensus about Susan's mother. Instead of finding himself on the opposing team when Susan begins to feel defensive about her mother, George opts to sympathize with the truth in what Susan is saying about her mother's loneliness. By doing this he is not just trying to come to consensus through criticism. He knows that to join with Susan in criticizing her mother, no matter how valid, will only get him into deep trouble. Once a couple stops being on opposite sides in these discussions, more productive solutions can be found. To achieve a consensus, the partner who is not the child of the "problem parent" must:

1. Listen for the defensive stance of your spouse.
2. At all costs, *do not attack* the parent or parents whom you are discussing, even if doing this seems to be mirroring your spouse's point of view. The minute you do this, the chance for consensus is lost.
3. Focus the discussion on what both of you can do to alleviate the tension that is being created.
4. Always remember that your spouse is the parent's child and, as such, has a vested interest in preserving and protecting the image of that parent.

Consensus-building is a critically important tool in any strong marriage. It ultimately affords a couple the ability to clearly assess and anticipate their parents and in-laws in ways that do not leave them at odds with each other. The goal of consensus-building is to bring couples to a common ground of understanding.

An Important Note: Many people enter marriage assuming that they can say anything they wish about their spouse or their spouse's family, and because their spouse loves them, he or she should be able to understand and accept it. Nothing could be farther from the truth. How you speak to your spouse may often require mammoth amounts of restraint and sensitivity. If you consider your spouse your most precious person in the world, it will naturally follow that you must nurture and protect his or her feelings. Therefore, consider the tone and attitude with which you speak. We all possess an enormous capacity to heal and support, but we also possess the ability to be destructive and nonproductive. Awareness of how you speak to each other is a most important factor in working toward consensus.

Fear of Confrontation

One of the biggest obstacles faced by couples who are beginning the work of coming to consensus is the fear that if they join with their spouse and agree about their parents' transgressions and idiosyncrasies, they will actually be called upon to *confront* them in some way. The fear of confrontation is one of the most powerful dynamics that keeps couples from unifying. The fear of losing or damaging the relationship with one's parents is so strong that a couple will often willingly endure terrible marital strife as the alternative to setting limits and facing potential conflict with their parents.

Tony, a 25-year-old mechanic, reported his fears this way:

"My mother and I have always been close, but she's a pretty demanding woman. I see her every Sunday with my wife, and I stop by there alone two or three times a week. That's what she wants. I know it makes her happy, so I do it. Lately my wife, Janice, has been after me to come home directly after work more often. At first she didn't mind my visits to my folks' house, but now she is annoyed that we don't have enough time together. She says that my mom has my dad there with her, and that she is home all alone if I don't get home. We've been arguing over this for weeks now, and I see Janice's point, but to tell you the truth, I'm a little afraid to bring it up with my mom. Last January she had a falling-out with my aunt over *nothing,* and now she's not speaking with her. My mom has made a habit of cutting people loose when she feels they've crossed her. This is *big,* and I'm afraid she'll take it the wrong way and stop talking to me."

Odele, a 34-year-old teacher who happens to be French, reports her fear this way:

"I am my husband's second wife. My mother-in-law, I've been told many times by her, just adored Erik's first wife and was heartbroken when the marriage broke up. I've been having a problem with her. She constantly puts down the work I do at the local French school and always manages to talk about how the French people were so unfriendly when she went to France fifteen years ago. All this talk gets on my nerves. Erik tells me he's tired of my complaining to him, that she doesn't mean it and that I should just turn a deaf ear. I don't feel supported by him, and I also know that if it goes the wrong way, she will use it against me for the rest of my days. Every time I bring it up, Erik gets colder and colder and I don't know what to do."

Tony and Odele's core fear is that they are facing some ultimate result, some permanent consequence if they take a stand and protect their marriages. Tony at least has the support of his wife; Odele is suffering without Erik's support. What Tony and Odele share is a willingness to let their marriages bear the pressure rather than to place the problem where it really belongs—with the parent or in-law. Their first step should be to look back in the Marriage Mirror so they can figure out how their attitudes on these issues were formed. Then they must make sure their allegiance to their spouses is in place. Finally, with the power of two, the couples must decide if they can face the most dire outcome together. Here lies the most important factor: If a couple is willing to face the worst possible outcome because they know that they are right, they have a much better chance of getting the parent to go along with the program.

Is it possible to confront parents without losing them? The answer is *yes*. The parents' fear of losing their child is a motivating factor that enables them to adapt to their child's "requirements." Many couples don't know this to be true, because they are too afraid to test the waters.

Is it possible to honestly assess our parents' behavior *without* having to confront them directly? Here, too, the answer is *yes*. Remember Phil and Robin in Chapter Three? They had to come to a consensus about Phil's parents' contact-hungry style. They never did confront Phil's parents about their behavior, but rather found the mutual understanding they gained by looking honestly at Phil's parents and the history of their own lack of support for each other was enough to take some of the pressure off their marriage.

From the Perspective of Laughter

"Family jokes, though rightly cursed by strangers, are the bond that keeps most families alive," wrote British author Stella Benson in her book *Pipers and a Dancer*.[11] After many years of consensus-building, couples report that they can speak about their parents' foibles and attitudes with something close to humor. Once the fear and taboo about looking at your parents realistically is removed, the discussion of their attitudes and behaviors can be downright hilarious. Developing private jokes about their parents and in-laws can help a couple get through a difficult dinner or a long family weekend. It also helps them to appreciate that some of what they find so difficult in their parents is really food for laughter rather than anger. If your goal is to make interaction with your parents a more pleasurable experience, or in some cases simply a less painful experience, humor can give you and your spouse a unifying language.

There are times when your spouse may be able to use humor directly with an offending parent or in-law. Dr. Evelyn Duvall, in her book *In-Laws: Pro and Con,* talks about a couple who have the husband's mother living with them. While they both work, she keeps house for them. Her entire life revolves around them, and her daughter-in-law finds the situation tension-filled. She feels her mother-in-law is petulant, interfering, and dependent. She goes on to describe an incident in which the daughter-in-law, upon returning home from work one day, was met with this barrage:

"Did you put on your rubbers? Are you sure you had your umbrella with you? Did you enjoy your food at lunchtime today?" The mother-in-law finally stopped herself short and said, "Here I am carrying on at you so, when I'm living off you, spending your money . . ."

At which, the daughter-in-law broke in with, "It isn't the money so much. You can have that, but will you just leave my soul alone!"

After this, with a twist of wry humor, the mother-in-law would catch herself in the midst of a fussing episode to ask, "Am I pinching your soul again?"

Forevermore, this daughter-in-law and mother-in-law have a humorous phrase that enables them to alert themselves to and unhook themselves from potential conflict, as well as show respect for each other.

The Warning Signs of Resistance

Clear signs of discord appear when a couple is avoiding, resisting, or simply losing the battle to reach consensus. Once a couple gets to know these signs, they can help each other check the lost ground and try again.

There are a few types of interactions that are clear indicators of lost consensus. If you can come to recognize these indicators, you will go a long way toward reopening discussion and building consensus. Sensitivity and patience is required on both sides of this discussion. We must realize that, like ourselves, our spouses respond like defensive children when asked to cast a publicly critical eye on a parent. It is an instinctive response left over from childhood, when each of us fought to preserve our view of our parents for the sake of our sense of security. Each child must see his or her parents as good, strong and all knowing, or else how could the child feel adequately protected in the larger world? You or your spouse should not be condemned if it takes one or both of you a while to learn how to "fight" this innate behavior.

The Pseudodisagreement

Gail, a 25-year-old law student, reported this classic pseudodisagreement.

> "We nearly got divorced before our wedding. My parents were paying for most of the wedding and they wanted to have no alcohol, since they are nondrinkers. Bruce's parents thought an open bar would be a more generous way of handling things, and they were, after all, paying for that portion of the wedding. In the early days of discussing the wedding, Bruce and I thought a champagne toast would be just the thing, since we don't drink much and neither do our friends. However, we developed an odd case of amnesia over this point as Bruce and I fought viciously . . . I defending my parents, and he defending his. We lost sight of ourselves and in the process nearly killed each other defending positions we didn't even hold. We almost always agree. That's one of the reasons I'm marrying Bruce!"

Here is a perfect example of how easy it is to lose consensus when the fear of confrontation, or of offending parents, surfaces. Gail and Bruce were suddenly unable to retrieve that sense of agreement. They *had* consensus about their own feelings toward this issue of alcohol at the wedding early on in their discussions. What they *hadn't* done was come to consensus about what they would do if they ran into conflict with their parents. They had not *anticipated* their parents' behavior and made a plan of action to respond to it. Before they knew it, they were lost in the mire of arguing without knowing what they were fighting for. Each was afraid and guilty about wanting something different from what their parents wanted and didn't want to hurt or offend anyone. Instead, they unconsciously opted to hurt each other rather than face confrontation or unpleasantness with either set of their parents.

The pseudodisagreement is a common form of argument between spouses. It is, in fact, a *false* argument. In these types of arguments, a couple usually is in agreement in principle or about the content, but the emotional travail of "going against" their parents' wishes leaves them fighting for positions that are not their own. This false disagreement is unconsciously created for the express purpose of avoiding conflict with their parents. If you find yourself defending positions that you do not hold for yourself, but are echoes of your parents' stance, you are engaged in a pseudodisagreement. Back up a moment to figure out what YOU are fighting for. It is not easy to let go of a position once you have held fast to it, even if it makes no real sense. If you can be honest with yourself and your spouse about getting caught up in defending your parents' position, you will begin to rediscover the consensus you lost.

Blaming and Character Assassination

Ben, a 55-year-old longshoreman, reported this exchange that has been going on with his wife, Dierdre, for years:

BEN: "Dad wants me to come by the garage on Saturday to fix the bumper on his old truck."

DIERDRE: "Why does he want to fix that old thing? What is it with him? Every Saturday he wants you over there to do something or other. It's a waste of your time, and I thought you had told him that you weren't going to help him with it."

BEN: "I never actually saw him to tell him. I was busy this week and never stopped by to go over it with him. Anyway, I thought I could go there for a couple of hours and help the old guy out."

DIERDRE: "Great! I thought we were going to shop for Ann's wedding gift on Saturday. But of course you can't say no to your daddy. Why don't you stand up to him like a real man?"

BEN: "What are you talking about? I say no plenty. Tell me you're so good at getting off the phone with your mother. You two talk a blue streak."

DIERDRE: "You never keep your word with me. I can't count on you for anything."

BEN: "You know, you are just hateful when it comes to my dad. You are so petty and stupid about him. What has he ever done to you?"

DIERDRE: "Nothing, that's the point. He doesn't care one bit about me or you, he just uses you to do his chores."

Well, you wouldn't think it possible that a man of 55 would be found calling his wife "stupid" or that a woman of 54 would be implying that her husband was not manly enough to say no to his daddy. But there it is. The moment they started blaming each other for Saturday's dilemma and assassinating each other's character with those few choice words, they had missed the boat. They should have heeded the "red flag" warning them that they were resisting dealing with the real issue. Clearly Ben's dad has a hold on him that makes it difficult for him to say no to him. But just as clearly, Dierdre's assertion that she can't count on Ben for anything is far from the truth. The real truth here is that they never came to a comfortable consensus about the pull Ben's dad has over him, and they never came to consensus about how they were going to handle it as a couple.

Let's see if we can't help them build some consensus and change blame and character assassination into a productive and unifying discussion:

BEN: "I think I'm going to go over on Saturday and help my dad fix the fender on the old truck."

DIERDRE: "I thought you had told him that you wouldn't do it . . . that it wasn't worth fixing."

BEN: "I never saw him this week to tell him. Anyway, I

thought I'd go over there for a couple of hours so that I could help the old guy out."

DIERDRE: "Look Ben, I know you really feel terrible if you don't go over when your dad asks you to, but we had agreed to going shopping for Ann's wedding gift on Saturday."

BEN: "Well, my Dad's old and he gets a lot of pleasure out of working on the truck."

DIERDRE: "I know he's almost impossible to say no to, but sometimes it is necessary because *we* have plans."

BEN: "What's a few hours?"

DIERDRE: "Ben, you are missing the point. It's not the few hours, although when you two get together you lose track of time. It's that we end up rearranging our life every time he calls. Of course you want to help him, but we need to find a way to do that and still have some time together when we have plans."

BEN: "He's old school. He just expects that what he wants he will get out of respect . . . he's the father."

DIERDRE: "And we should show him that respect, but there must be a way to do that without always jumping every time he calls, and missing out on our time together. I personally think that he wouldn't mind you saying 'not today' if you could offer him another date right then and there. Then he would know you are willing to do it and you respect his request . . . just not right at that moment."

BEN: "I can't imagine his understanding it."

DIERDRE (smiling): "I bet you can't even imagine yourself *saying* it."

BEN (laughing): "I think my knees would shake!"

This second dialogue shows how hard Dierdre worked to help her husband see that he was ostensibly "afraid" to disappoint his father or be what he perceived as disrespectful. He has been responding all his life to his father's credo, "Father = Respect = Compliance." By working hard to keep focused on Ben's and his father's interaction rather than her own angry disappointment, she was able to move Ben gently along in the conversation. She was even able to stay poised enough to interject a little levity into the discussion. The image of Ben's knees shaking as he approaches his dad has the potential of becoming a "private joke" that helps them through the difficult act of setting limits on his father.

Passive Resistance

Fay, a 39-year-old secretary, and her husband, Keith, a 37-year-old computer programmer, thought they had come to consensus about what to do when Keith's parents tried to monopolize them. They had been really good about talking through their resistance and developing a plan of action that would enable them to minimize the unreasonable demands on their time. They had agreed to brunch on every other Sunday. Even though this felt like a lot to them because they had to drive an hour each way, they were able to realize that in his parents' eyes, this contact was the bare minimum. Sounds good. Looks good on paper. There was only one problem: Keith and Fay were late every Sunday.

At first they were able to attribute this to the length of their drive, the traffic situation, or the difficult task of rounding up the children and getting them out of the house on time. After a while, however, their excuses began to wear thin. Keith began to experience a niggling feeling as these Sundays approached that he had so much to do around the house that he couldn't spare the time. He never really shared this thought with Fay. Fay was starting to experience a concern that the children were returning home so late on Sunday evening that they were tired for school the next day. She never shared this thought with Keith. For their part, Keith's parents started to up the ante and suggest that they sleep over Saturday night at their house so that they wouldn't have to rush and take that long drive twice in one day. Keith and Fay felt that long arm of his parents wrapping around them in what they perceived to be a stranglehold. Their arrival times got later and later, increasing the tension.

But they had landed themselves in this tub of hot water. Ostensibly they had agreed to the regular brunches, but unconsciously and passively they were acting out their resistance to the plan. It is important for couples to think realistically when they enter into agreements with their parents. They must plumb the depths of their motives and wishes in order to know why they are agreeing to a plan and if they are willing to follow it through with commitment. Passive resistance is hard to recognize at first, because it doesn't have the blaring noise of argument attached to it. It can take a while for a couple to recognize their part in creating additional pressure on their marriage through passively resisting the plans they make with their parents. Ironically enough, passive resistance is a form of avoidance that is active, determined, enterprising, and undeniably designed to defer direct confrontation. It gets its name simply because it allows couples to enter into a pact without having to actively acknowledge their intent.

It is easier to identify passive resistance if only one member of the couple is behaving in that way. If, in this case, Keith had been comfortable with the agreement he had made with his folks, but Fay had been passively resisting, she would have been the one to dally and dawdle despite her protestations that she agreed to the plan. As the family arrival times got later, there would have been eventual conflict between her and Keith. Then clearly the pressure brought to bear on Keith as a result of her conduct could lead to skirmishes and real dissension. Then, they might notice that they had a problem on their hands and work toward a consensus. In the case of Keith and Fay, they had to work harder to see how they were resisting their agreed-upon plan. Then they had to work toward a new consensus concerning how and when to be with his folks.

A Conspiracy of Silence

Niles, a 48-year-old vice principal at an elementary school, reports this:

> "My mother-in-law is a formidable woman. She is large and loving and kind of barrels her way through life. We all love her, especially my children. She is the kind of woman who can wrap all three of them in one embrace! When she visits us she cooks, cleans, gets on the floor and plays with the kids, and is pretty good-natured. She takes over, but with such good intent it's almost hard to say there is a downside to all of this. The only real complaint I have is that the gifts she brings the kids are way too costly. I don't mean that they are a bit over the edge, they are *way* over the edge. Also she doesn't consult us about what she is bringing with her. Last week she brought a 20-inch color TV for my oldest to keep in his room. Frankly, I don't believe in kids having their own TVs and I was annoyed that she went ahead and did it without talking to us. I didn't say anything at the time. When I caught Joyce's eye and made a face, she shushed me. I ended up going down to my workshop and working off my annoyance by sanding and hammering. After all, she's my mother-in-law, not my mother."

When Niles was asked what his wife thought, he said he imagined that she didn't mind his mother-in-law's extravagances as much as he did. He thought she was softer with the kids anyway. So, we asked her. Joyce responded this way:

> "My mother is great with the kids. She's a much better grandmother than she was a mother. When I was grow-

ing up, she was stern and had so much to do that I don't remember her often playing with us. We had money, but my dad was frugal and we had very few luxuries. I guess that's how he managed to amass the money he left to my mother when he died. I just love the way she is with our kids . . . sort of like I'm getting loved too. I think the gifts are way out of line with what I feel is appropriate. At those moments I feel that she has overstepped her position, but I've never said anything because overall she is so good with the kids and to us that it would seem somehow ungrateful. Also, I imagine she is spending the money that my dad never let her spend and it gives her so much pleasure. I hate to take away any of her happiness and, frankly, I don't want to lose any of the good feeling that has developed between us these past few years. Niles doesn't say anything, so I figure he doesn't mind too much."

Niles was surprised to hear that Joyce shared his feelings about his mother-in-law's out-of-bounds spending on the kids. They had entered into a conspiracy of silence without realizing it. They had ignored their growing discontent with the situation. This "madness" went on for a number of reasons. Joyce was always playing back the deprivation that her mother put up with during her years with her father. She felt sorry for her, and so she subjugated her own values about the gifts in order to meet her mother's imagined wishes. Niles had abdicated. He assumed that because she was Joyce's mother, only Joyce had the right to decide how to handle the situation. They both feared that Joyce's mother would be angry and hurt if they brought up the problem. They had ceded their responsibility as parents. They responded to Joyce's mother by hoping the problem would go away if they just ignored it. Through open discussion, they realized that they shared the same view; it was just their motives for remaining silent that were different. Only now could they possibly offer each other enough strength and enough backup to raise the issue tactfully with Joyce's mother.

Another important contributing factor in creating the conspiracy of silence was the use of *assumption*. They each had assumed they knew how their spouse was feeling about the situation. However, each had assumed incorrectly. Many couples think that if they are really close to each other, they don't have to express themselves, but rather each spouse should be able to read the other person's mind and know what he or she is thinking and feeling.

There is no basis in fact for this theory. No matter how close a couple becomes, no matter how many sentences of your spouse's you are able to complete, no matter how often you can anticipate his or her next word, you cannot rely on divination for the truth. The rule of thumb is: Assume you know nothing. That way, your discussions will not be further hindered by what you imagine your spouse to be thinking or feeling. Asking simple questions, checking out your assumptions, and clarifying your positions can help you avoid feeling isolated from each other on difficult issues.

Consensus-building, the use of humor, watching for the warning signals of resistance—these are the essential tools for couples who wish to remove unnecessary pressures from their marriage. These are the tools for mature couples who wish to enter into a positive relationship with their parents, free of fear and full of the constructive power that resides in every marriage.

CHAPTER SIX

The Judicious Use of Power

*"Power has only one duty . . . to secure the social
welfare of the people."*
Benjamin Disraeli[12]

Tact, sensitivity, and the judicious use of power are the
cornerstones of building a relationship with parents and
in-laws that provides joy and companionship. All the understanding that a couple has gleaned from looking at themselves in the Marriage Mirror, accepting the power that
resides in their marriage, and coming to consensus about
their parents must now be transformed into action. You
must now venture forth and change the way you speak to
and approach your parents. Having a new repertoire of
things to say and do will result in different and less stressful
interactions with your parents. Before we discuss actual scenarios and strategies, let's pause for a moment to alert ourselves to the ever-present array of obstacles that stand in the
way of taking action and making change.

Guilty As Charged

How potent is guilt? The word comes from the Old English *gylt*, which meant "crime." The *American Heritage Dictionary of the English Language* defines guilt as self-reproach for supposed inadequacy or wrongdoing. For many couples, the very act of presenting their needs and requirements as a couple to their parents is tantamount to committing a crime. But if you look at the definition, the word *supposed* leaps out. Though they may seem decidedly real to a couple, these "supposed wrongdoings" may not be as real as they think. Are they really committing a crime when they want a weekend free to be with their own children and spouse? Are they due for a court appearance when they refuse their parents' generous offer to take them along on vacation with them and their parents pout for the next two weeks? Are they really deserving of a jail sentence because they decided that having all four grandparents at their son's bowling party would be too confusing, so they told them they couldn't come . . . and the grandparents were *not* delighted! Put this way, of course it seems ridiculous. But when you are living through the actual moment of taking a stand, there is no reminder of the absurdity of your feelings. There is only this all-absorbing, gut feeling that you have done something terribly wrong and that you are irreparably hurting your parents.

How do you get so much guilt? Guilt is created when there is a clash between the real and imagined expectations of your family and your own adult wishes. These family expectations may have been passed down from generation to generation like the antique rocker in your living room that you cherish so much. They may be newly formed expectations that are born out of a change in the status of one of your parents (for example, the death of a spouse or a move to your city). It is when the grown children experience their own desires as being in conflict with their parents' that they come face to face with that all too familiar guilty feeling.

Guilt comes up most frequently when a couple expresses, through their actions and words, that they expect to have a life of their own. The guilt is especially potent if any of the parents are living unfulfilled lives themselves and are substituting their children's lives for their own. Guilt also arises easily when a couple feels that they are distressing their parents in any way. But R. D. Laing may have been on the right track in his book *The Self and Others* when he pointed out: "True guilt is guilt at the obligation one owes to oneself *to be* oneself. False guilt is guilt felt at not being what other people feel one ought to be or assume that one is."[13] Clearly he is speaking of the healthy drive to be oneself and have one's own life.

Overall, guilt is a useless emotion. It stops couples from taking action, it leaves important words unsaid, and it stymies attempts of couples and their parents to reach the higher ground of mutual understanding. It is hard to rid yourself of guilt once it has become part of the emotional repertoire in your relationship with your parents. It is cold comfort for some to realize that standing up for what is right for your marriage is natural and human. Guilt is such a painful, almost mind-blurring emotion. However, with the support of your spouse, the next time you express your needs, the next time you say no to a parent, ask yourself if your self-inflicted punishment really fits the crime!

On the Altar of Sacrifice

"Too long a sacrifice
Can make a stone of the heart"
William Butler Yeats[14]

Civilized as we are, we still practice the rite of human sacrifice. Hasn't this practice long been outlawed? Indeed, but couples still engage in this ancient ritual without being cognizant of their own horrifying behavior. Couples frequently offer up their marriages as sacrifices on the altar of their parents' demands and wishes. Remember Karen the faint of heart and her fiancé Victor the Trailblazer from Chapter Two? There was a situation where Karen almost sacrificed her marriage to Victor to keep her parents from the distress they would feel if their once sickly daughter ventured out into the world and lived a little! Victor saw the sacrifice she was considering, and it made him angry. He lent that outrage to Karen, and she was able to use it to jettison herself into her new life. Lo and behold, her parents survived!

A sense of hopelessness arises in children when they can't rescue their parents from the distress they feel they are causing them. This gets transformed into a marital or self-sacrifice that is designed to take the place of the parents' suffering. Marital sacrifices are most prevalent in families where the parents have either devoted themselves in some extreme way to their child over many years, or are high-voltage parents, or where the emotional distress level runs high and children are working to diffuse it.

William Butler Yeats wisely stated that sacrifice that goes on too long causes a hardening of the heart. Ultimately, too much sacrifice can turn to anger. Often it is first manifested and expressed by the one spouse. This is where the conflict arises for the couple. It is necessary to come to consensus about how much they can, as a couple, willingly sacrifice to their parents. Compromise will be essential, because the underpinnings of sacrifice run deep and may take a while to undo.

Making sacrifices for your family and sacrificing your marriage are two different things. All family members have obligations that they must meet by dint of being in a family. A sick parent, a lonely aunt, picking up the work of a holiday after parents become too old to handle it and, most of all, respect are part and parcel of family life. Meeting the obligations of being a member of a family gives richness and depth to relationships and offers opportunities for generations to mingle and enjoy each other. There are naturally times when a couple will have to put themselves out for a family member, or take on an unwanted task, simply because there is no one else to do it. But if a couple is working all the time at supporting each other, coming to consensus, and making sure that they preserve time for their marital life, family obligations and sacrifices can be made without sacrificing their marriage.

Emotional Storms

Finally there is fear—fear of the emotional storms that often accompany a couple's taking a stand on behalf of their own marriage. Some parents see nothing wrong with pulling out all the stops and playing every emotional card in their hand to sidetrack a couple's attempts at defining themselves and their needs. Parents often relate to their grown children and in-law children in much the same way that parents do with young children. They feel entitled to say whatever pops into their heads without regard for the couple as equal adults. Some parents and in-laws have been known to use anger, emotional tantrums, pouting, and all forms of manipulation in their interactions with their grown children. Couples often wish to avoid the emotional wear and tear of these exchanges. But there is hope. If a couple learns to exercise the inherent power in their marriage, to express their position diplomatically and live through their parents' potential emotional tantrums, they can set themselves free. They will discover, as has been mentioned before, that parents rarely are willing to forfeit their relationships with their children. More often than not, they will adapt to the stand the couple makes. This takes fortitude and unity on the part of the couple, but it can be done.

Skills and Strategies

*"It is not a bad thing that children should
occasionally, and politely, put parents
in their place."*
Colette[15]

What Can They Expect From Us?

The first aspect of learning to approach parents and in-laws in ways that preserve your marital integrity involves *clarity*. A couple must use consensus-building as a way to gain a clear idea of exactly what their parents can expect from them. This calls on a couple to develop a *family approach* to when, where, and with whom they wish to spend their time. This calls on them to know how much sacrifice they can make without compromising their marriage. This calls on them to determine where the joy lies in their relationships with their parents and how to maximize *those* contacts. This calls on them to use the art of anticipation to calculate, before an event, their parents' needs and expectations. They must work together to decide just how they will meet or modify those expectations. All this is necessary and more. For every couple knows what it feels like to have their parents throw them a curve ball, and every couple must learn what to do in those circumstances.

The Plenary Meeting

Before we look at the different approaches that can be taken to change thought into action, we must take note of the importance of a plenary meeting—a meeting attended by all qualified members. (Plenary means "complete in all respects.") When a couple has a plenary meeting to determine the best course of action to take, they are recognizing the importance of each member of the couple as qualified and essential to the decision-making process. These are meetings that take place at times set aside during which couples determine the best course to follow when they present information to their parents and in-laws. At these meetings a couple can work on such issues as consensus-building; deciding who will approach the parents, and when and how the approach will take place; the most diplomatic way to convey the information; and others. Plenary meetings can take place over a meal, in the car, or in front of the fireplace, but they *must* occur in order for a couple to truly take action from a unified position.

Worst-Case Scenarios

Often a good way to begin a plenary meeting is to ask the question, "What is the worst possible outcome that will occur if we take a stand and hold firm?" For most couples, the practical answer to that question can range from "Not much will happen" to "My parents would never speak to me again." The vast majority of couples who look realistically at this question find their answers falling somewhere between those two extremes.

Gail and Bruce, the young couple from Chapter Five who were having a pseudodisagreement over the alcoholic beverages to be served at their wedding, might like to ask themselves this question. At a plenary meeting, they could discuss the range of worst-case scenarios—everything from the parents pulling out and refusing to pay for the wedding to emotional outbursts from Bruce's parents should be considered. How bad could all this *actually* get? Often a couple's unspoken fears loom large, but once they are examined realistically in the light of day, they are either identified as unfounded, or the actual truth of what might happen is found to be not nearly the catastrophe their imaginations have concocted. It is important to explore all the possibilities, no matter how absurd.

Pam, a new homeowner, reported this worst-case scenario:

"Jack and I had just bought our new house, and I went out looking for living room drapes. I must have spent days handling material and struggling over the decision . . . mind you, it wasn't because I was worried about what Jack might like, but rather I worried about what my mother would think. She's a part-time interior designer. I finally made my decision, and Jack loved the drapes. We arranged to have an open house to show our relatives the new place, but as the day approached I started to become anxious and upset. I fought with Jack over the slightest thing, began accusing him of not participating in decisions, of being an absentee husband. By the time the day rolled around, I was eyeing those drapes with mistrust. Had I made the right decision? Would my mother like them? What would she do if she didn't? And most important, why hadn't Jack taken a real interest in the decorating?"

After much discussion about what the worst possible outcome would be that day, Pam was able to say that deep down she feared that her mother would embarrass her in front of everyone. She was also tense because she had succeeded in alienating Jack over the past few days with her wild accusations and anger. When asked how her mother might embarrass her, Pam responded by laughing. She said that her worst fear was that her mom would walk up to the curtains and tear them off the windows. Her next fear was that in a loud voice in front of everyone, her mother would say something devastating to her about her taste in drapes. Finally, she imagined some offhand slight at Jack, since he had agreed to the choice of drapes.

If Pam's mother responded in any of these imagined ways, the behavior would only serve to make her mother look immature, tactless, and absurd. Though it might be embarrassing to them, Pam's mother's behavior would not reflect on her and Jack, their taste, or their maturity. It would do nothing to Jack's and Pam's reputations. When asked again if she and Jack were in accord over the drapes, Pam responded adamantly that they both loved them. It was recommended that she return home to Jack and explain to him why she had been so difficult and quarrelsome over the past few days—and to apologize to him. Taken out of the position of trying-to-please child and placed in the role of wife and united partner, she was able to feel stronger about meeting any potential storm created by her mother. She was also able to laugh at the absurdity of some of the concerns she had about her mother's behavior. Looking at worst-case scenarios often can leave you doubled up with laughter.

On the other hand, looking closely at these possible outcomes can leave some couples with a genuine awareness of how intractable and extreme their parents might be in a given situation. Some parents allow themselves to react to circumstances by either digging in their heels or by manipulating those around them, making everyone uncomfortable. For couples who deal with these types of parents or in-laws, their sense of hopelessness at ever being able to take a stand and effect an adaptation in their parents is real. Later in this chapter we will discuss these intractable parents and the effect they can have on a marriage. We also will discuss "damage control," an approach useful to couples in limiting the negative effect and pressure such parents bring to bear on a marriage.

"We'll Get Back to You"

We've all been caught off guard by a parent who tells us things like "Oh, by the way, I've told Aunt Sylvia that we will meet her for dinner Saturday night before she leaves to go back home to Texas." Your head spins for a moment. You are a corporate executive with a working wife and three children. You may have plans for that evening, may need to arrange a baby-sitter in advance if you even want to attend this unplanned gathering, and you haven't had a chance to talk it over with your wife yet. But in the eyes of your mother, you are still the child she can tell to wash his hands and brush his teeth. She glides effortlessly back into the role of arranger of your life, for it is a role she has perfected over so many years!

Pressure to respond to her either with a fit of pique or with acquiescence may feel compelling to you at that moment, but it is always better not to give in to the temptation to respond instinctively. Rein in your rage, hold back your histrionics, and be absolutely sure to contain your consent! Simply employ a phrase that will free you to have *time to think* about what you and your spouse want to do in the situation. Truthfully say, *"We will have to get back to you about that."*

Seems simple enough . . . but like every change in a person's behavior, it takes thought and practice. It also takes courage to be able to say those words while looking into the eyes of your baffled parents. After all, the very fact that they had gone ahead and made plans for you without your knowledge means that they are hardly expecting their "invitation" to be refused. Letting the statement *"We will have to get back to you"* hang in the air, and not blithering to fill the moments of discomfort that may follow them, is another courageous act necessary in making this work. Remember, you have the *right* to decide *as a couple* exactly how you will be spending your time. You are entitled to have *time to think*. You concurrently have an obligation to restrain yourself from reacting like a petulant and angry child when responding to your parents. If you fall into that trap, you are setting yourself up to be treated like a child.

Early Warning Systems

Often couples will run into enormous backlash once they begin to assert themselves. They find that parents, instead of relinquishing their hold, hang on tighter and pursue them with more vigor than ever before. If, for a moment, you think about it from your parents' perspective, you will be able to understand why. For all intents and purposes, when you marry, your parents experience a loss. They no longer have exclusive claim to your affections, and you no longer require their frequent ministrations. So as a couple begins the process of asserting themselves as a unit, parents may feel increasingly bereft.

In an attempt to establish the "Royal We," couples will sometimes clumsily employ the word "no" to establish boundaries and set limits. For some parents, hearing the word "no" leaves them with the sense that "never" is what you really meant to say. This of course can send them into a frenzy of action to ensure that they will still have you, that they are still important to you. At these times the best way for a couple to reduce the onslaught of requests for their time and company is to employ the use of the word "no" with a qualifier. If parents feel that "no" means just this time and not always and forever, they can cope much better with the disappointment of not having your attentions when they want them. If you can anticipate with your parents the next time that they will see you or speak with you, you are limiting their disappointment to one event, and you have given them the hope and prospect of future times together. It seems curious that you would need to do this, but parents experience tremendous anxiety when faced with the prospect of losing contact or control over a child, no matter how old that child may be. It is surely a small price to pay for being able to have a more relaxed and enjoyable time with your parents.

Early Warning Systems can be set in place for almost any situation. Couples with ongoing conflicts with their families over where to spend holidays may use a yearly Early Warning System. For one couple, their Early Warning System took the form of a statement about the upcoming year's arrangements. In a plenary meeting, they wrote down each major event from birthdays to Christmas and New Year's. They sent out a sheet of paper to their parents with these instructions: "We have attempted to divide our time fairly between both families. We know that there will be disappointments when you look at this, but you can be sure that next year we will be reversing this list so we might have the opportunity of spending the important days of the year with everyone. We will be sticking to these plans, barring unforeseen circumstances. We look forward to being together! Do not lose this paper!"

What a creative solution! And this tactic alleviated all the bickering they had been doing with each other. It helped them not only to deal fairly with their parents, but with each other as well. They each had their own ideas of how much time to spend with their own parents. They had to "duke it out" *themselves* before sending that note. Had they sent the list on to their parents without having completely negotiated with each other, without having worked out their own preferences first, without *total* clarity, they would have folded at the first obstacle thrown their way by their parents. The strength they found in each other through the process of coming to consensus made it easier for them to face what might come. They stopped trying to make everyone happy all the time, an impossible task that left them exhausted and angry with each other. They *acknowledged* to their parents, up front, that there would be some disappointments in the arrangements. Indeed, as they were formulating the list, the spouses each experienced disappointment at having to change their own old family routines. Neither one wanted to give up their family's classic Christmas party or their mother's perfect Thanksgiving turkey, even if it was only for a year. But they acted as mature adults and worked through their struggles together rather than in front of their parents. The list gave their parents the *reassurance* that not only did they wish to see them, but they could *count* on seeing them. They *anticipated* their parents' dissatisfaction with the plan and assured them that they would be reversing their appearances the following year. Anticipation, acknowledgment, and reassurance are the hallmarks of a good Early Warning System.

Speaker of the House

> *"Speak for Yourself . . . John Alden."*
> John Smith

Once consensus is reached, the "Speaker of the House" must be chosen. *Who* will do the talking for the couple? Couples often make the spurious connection in their minds that if their spouse speaks up for them it shows fealty, loyalty, and devotion. Though, in fact, all of these assumptions might be somewhat correct, when it comes to determining a Speaker of the House, more than just a "show" of allegiance and loyalty must be the guiding force. Deciding who will do the talking must be based on a few important considerations:

What is the problem at hand?
What are the couple's goals in making an intervention?
Which spouse has the conflict?
Which spouse is putting up resistance?
Who will the parents most likely listen to?
Who might disarm the parents by being a novel person to interact with them around this issue?

Looking back on Richard and Beth from Chapter Three, we see a classic wish for one of the spouses to do the talking, but for all the wrong reasons. Beth's father "jokingly" put Richard down. Richard felt that Beth was never able to stand up to her father and take his side. He was furious with her because she wouldn't show her allegiance to him by defending him. Richard believed that further evidence of her father's hold over her were her attacks on Richard that immediately followed visits to her father's home.

When they looked at the problem of Beth's dad putting Richard down, they shared the perception (possibly correct) that Beth's dad showed no respect for Richard. Conflict arose within the couple because each was hoping the other would take care of the problem; consequently, they had not formulated a plan of action between them. Once they discussed the issue, they came to a consensus. Their goal was for her father to show more respect and to stop making jokes at Richard's expense. Their goal was also for Richard to feel more supported by Beth. They believed that if Beth were designated as Speaker of the House on this issue, then her father, who obviously loved and admired her, would "hear better" and be more receptive to her pleas that Richard be treated with more respect. But they didn't realize that this was the wrong choice.

Richard's assumption that only Beth could get him "in" with her dad may be the exact reason that her father showed him little respect. Why wasn't he taking a stand on his own? Why wasn't *he* having a discussion with his father-in-law that spoke to the way he was being treated? Why was he waiting for Beth to pave the way and rescue him? By waiting, he was only perpetuating the image of himself as unable to take care of his own business. By hoping Beth would do it for him, he was potentially falling short in her eyes as well. It is natural for couples to assume that the person who should be the Speaker is the child most closely related to the side of the family with whom they are having a conflict. Though the blood-related child is often the Speaker of choice, it is not always the case—and less frequently than you might think.

More discussion brought this couple to yet another consensus:

your way through, taking the consequences as they came. Well, as a couple you can no longer afford either one of these stances. Why? Because if you botch this up, your *spouse* will naturally be the one blamed for *forcing* you to do this. Though you may be in the clear, the attack on your spouse will throw your marriage back into conflict.

Learning to *reserve* some thoughts and information seems impossible to many couples because they think it means *lying* to their parents. This is certainly not the case. There are many reasons, and good ones, for couples to carefully dole out information:

1. As a couple you are entitled to private thoughts, actions, and desires.
2. As adults, who want to be treated as such, telling *all* to your parents is generationally inappropriate because it feeds the notion that you are still answerable to your parents as a young child would be.
3. Parents who are naturally protective of their own have been known to take sides in a conflict between spouses. Parents often can't let go of their own distress over the conflict and continue harping and blaming your spouse for things long ago resolved between you.
4. As children, grown or otherwise, you are mandated to approach your parents respectfully. Diplomatic delivery of information allows you to convey your needs and desires without hurting or alienating your parents.

Let's look at Drake and Alice once again to see how their information can be shared diplomatically.

Though Alice is designated Speaker of the House on this issue, that doesn't leave Drake off the hook in terms of deciding exactly how their decision will be conveyed. These were the issues about which they could agree:

1. Drake and Alice's allegiance had to lie clearly with each other and their baby.
2. Constant unexpected visits threw off the baby's schedule.
3. They had to acknowledge that Drake's mother was not deliberately trying to make things difficult, but rather was naturally smitten with the baby and couldn't get enough of her.
4. Cutting Drake's mother off without regard for her feelings would result in her being offended, create a terrible rift in the family, and ultimately force them to move from their apartment in order to control their own lives.
5. Alice and Drake had the right to control the boundaries of their realm and define when foreigners could pass through their checkpoints.

They decided to handle it this way:

Alice invited her mother-in-law to come to visit on a specific afternoon for lunch and to play with the baby. She began by making offhand comments about the baby's sleep schedule and how delicate it had been of late. She also spoke of how she needed to catch forty winks herself when the baby rested, since they were often up a good deal of the night together. As she expected, her mother-in-law was all sympathy and understanding. It was then that Alice took the plunge. She first expressed to her mother-in-law how much pleasure it gave her that the baby and she got on so well. She talked of how she could imagine a future when the two of them (grandma and granddaughter) would be doing things together. (*Always speak of the positives, if you can, before setting a limit.*) Then she paused and said, "I've made an error in calculating just how much company and help I can enjoy and make use of right now, and I've got a favor to ask of you." Would she mind calling before she wanted to come over to see how the day was going and whether the baby and she were fit for visitors? True to form, at this point Drake's mother exclaimed that *she* wasn't a *visitor* but rather was *family*. She didn't mind if Alice was in a nightgown or unshowered. Alice didn't need to put on a show for her. Momentarily Alice was thrown off, but she regrouped and replied that they were asking this of *all* their relatives and friends for the sake of the baby. For the sake of the baby— no grandmother could resist this entreaty.

Rather than get into an argument, Alice moved quickly to change the subject. Her mother-in-law had heard the edict. She didn't like it and would have to digest it, but Alice didn't need to help her do that. *It was up to Drake's mother to make peace with the couple's decision.* Alice lightheartedly chatted throughout the afternoon, showing her mother-in-law gifts that had arrived for the baby and asking her advice about one baby lotion versus another. (*Alice was normalizing the request by not spending too much time on it, and she was showing her mother-in-law that she and her opinion still counted.*)

Never once during the afternoon did Alice refer to her mother-in-law's intrusiveness in a negative way. Never once did Alice single out her mother-in-law for her behavior. Throughout the afternoon, Alice peppered her talk with honest compliments and truthful promises of future connection. One might say that by not confronting her mother-in-law, Alice wasn't telling the truth. But in fact, Alice *was* telling the truth; she just wasn't sharing *all* of her and Drake's thinking on the matter with her mother-in-law. She was approaching her mother-in-law with the respect she deserved. As true adults, Drake and Alice realized that his mother's intrusions were more a matter of personal style than a deliberate act of aggression toward them.

Whew! Alice had done it! When she closed the apartment door as her mother-in-law left, she heaved a sigh of relief. It was over, and it had been taken care of—what a great feeling. However, it wasn't over, and the phone call to Drake from his mother later that day confirmed this. His mother paged him at the hospital and basically described the afternoon with the baby. Then she proceeded to say that Alice looked tired and was requesting that she call before she came over. Humbug! She thought a better idea would be if she came over and took the baby off Alice's hands so she could get some rest.

Now it was time for Drake to show some support. His mother was clearly trying to get back in through a "side door." She figured that Drake could be coaxed into convincing Alice that her own plan was the better one. Having *anticipated* this response from his mother, Drake heard his mother's comments for what they were and flew into action. He said that he also really wanted Alice to get some rest, and though his mother's offer was magnanimous, he knew Alice really well, and knew that she wouldn't get any real sleep with someone else padding about the house. She would feel compelled to make sure that other person was comfortable and had something to drink and eat, ultimately depriving herself of the much-needed rest. "No," he said, "I think our idea of having people call to check first is the best way for Alice and the baby to find the rest and routine they need." *Our idea* is the operative part of the phrase. It let his mother know that he and Alice had formed an alliance about this issue and that it was coming as no surprise to him. It also showed the full weight of his support for the plan.

Important Note: At no time did Drake or Alice single out his mother as a problem, or say anything to her that would make her feel hurt. They spoke solely from the point of view of their needs and the needs of the baby. By casting no blame, they avoided a futile argument about who is right or wrong in the situation. They accept that Drake's mother may not concur, but that they have the right to make the rules. They recognized that all she has to do is *adapt* rather than *agree*.

Owning Up to Your Responsibility

Another important part of approaching parents and being heard by them is making sure that you take responsibility for your part in the situation. Alice opened the conversation by clearly saying that she had misjudged her own ability to accept help and company at this time. That was a tactful way of saying that she and Drake had not set proper limits on boundary crossings. She took responsibility without too much "mea culpa," thus allowing the couple to acknowledge their role in the situation without having to act like guilty children. Learning to begin the dialogue by speaking of your own participation in the dilemma leaves parents freer to hear without defensiveness, to listen with sympathy, and to watch true adults in action.

Holding Your Ground

You've had plenary meetings, you've chosen your Speaker of the House, you've delivered your decision diplomatically with calm and respect, and you have offered your spouse the essential support. Now what? *You must hold your ground!*

Imagine if Drake's mother had not taken the news of their decision as well as she did. She only advanced on the boundary once, with Drake over the phone. Let's assume that she found it in her heart to pull out the big guns and informed Drake that he must have been brainwashed by Alice. What if she had implied that the apartment was really hers, and so she should be allowed to wander the rooms freely whenever she chose? What if she began disparaging Alice? Whether you are called brainwashed, henpecked, manipulated, or just a fool, *hold your ground!* When a parent mentions what you and your spouse consider to be the worst-case scenario, *hold your ground.* You will no doubt feel the sand shifting beneath your feet. No matter how justified you feel in your position, you will be standing in the middle of an emotional storm, and that is not an easy place to be. However, when you weather it, and you both survive, you will feel empowered. What your parents are doing is simply expressing their disappointment over your decision and possibly over your newfound unity. But disappointment is merely an emotion, and it will pass if you wait long enough and remain firmly resolved. You will see that indeed most parents don't disintegrate over an issue, that they do not abandon you or disinherit you. Usually all they do is talk big and sulk. If you truly believe that your position is justified, then you can support yourselves through this period. Huddling together against the emotional storm outside can be a very unifying experience for a couple.

The next thing to watch out for is your own guilt, an undermining culprit if ever there was one. As explained earlier in this chapter, guilt is formed when a couple's adult wishes appear to be counter to the perceived or real interest of their parents. It rears its head when a couple feels that they have caused parents distress. But does the punishment you are meting out to yourselves really fit the crime? It is important to remember that if you calmly and respectfully issue royal decrees that are reasonable, you need not get caught up in feeling guilty. If you issue royal decrees while casting blame and anger toward your parents, their distressed response will cause you some guilt and, more important, you will not have accomplished your mission. You will have acted like a petulant child, and will end up walking away from the interaction with them no better off and guilty to boot.

Intractable Parents Requiring Damage Control

Your parents won't budge. No matter how masterfully you wield your power, no matter how diplomatically you and your spouse approach them, no matter how unified a front you present, they cannot be moved! Some parents, by dint of either ignorance or sheer obstinacy, feel no need to compromise. They neither adapt nor understand. They make the lives of their children difficult and often impossible by failing to see reason or accept the power that resides in the couple. Having intractable parents often leaves a couple blaming each other for not making things different. It often causes them to argue over circumstances that cannot be changed, and, in general, keeps the misery level high between them.

"Damage control" frequently becomes the watchword for couples in this unfortunate situation. The couple must control the amount of internal havoc that this type of parents can perpetrate. First you must recognize that, indeed, you have such parents. Be careful, though, for there is danger in *mis*labeling your parents as this type of people. Some couples call their parents intractable as an easy way out. "What's the use in telling them anything or trying to change things? They'll never change." Writing them off in this way lets the couple off the hook. If, however, those parents are not really intractable, taking the easy way out precludes the possibility of improved relations that comes when efforts are made to have honest exchanges and set reasonable marital boundaries.

So, what do intractable parents really act like? First, though they may say that what they are doing is out of love for you both, their lack of respect and response when you issue royal decrees or express marital needs speaks otherwise. Second, they will almost always attempt to play an emotional trump card. They are willing to manipulate and maneuver to get their way, no matter the cost to you both. Third, they threaten and use parental power to keep you beholden and bewildered. Their love comes only if you play it their way. Threats about "the will" or "not taking the grandkids overnight" or simply "You'll never see us again" are part of the intractable parents' repertoire.

It is of the utmost importance that a couple never label their parents intractable until they have attempted on numerous occasions to diplomatically exert themselves as a couple. However, having done this and finding a brick wall at every turn, it is time for a couple to begin the practice of damage control.

Once you finally label your parents intractable, a period of relief follows. For the first time, you have defined behavior that has been tying you in knots for years. No more do you have to take this behavior to heart. No more do you have to blame each other for a parent's conduct. No more will you be putting pressure on your spouse, because you will no longer assume that if only your spouse were strong enough, he or she could stop his or her parents from behaving in this way. When the relief passes, it is replaced by the disappointment and sadness that comes from knowing that your parents, for whatever their reasons, cannot see their way clear to treat you like adults and put your marital needs before their own desires, even every now and again.

Damage control takes many forms. For some couples, it means severely limiting contact with their parents. For others, it means cutting them off completely. For some, it means developing a sense of humor about them and thus defusing the power that these parents have. The main thrust of damage control is to *limit the internal strife* that dealing with these parents often fosters in a marriage. Whatever a couple's course of action, it must, of course, emerge out of consensus and mutual support. Whatever a couple needs to do to handle this type of parents is fine so long as it maintains the integrity of their marriage and doesn't require aggressive retaliation against the parents.

One final important note as we wrap up this chapter: It is imperative that when issuing royal decrees and discussing marital priorities, your goal as a couple is for your parents to *adapt enough* so that the quality of your time together is improved. The idea that you must make your parents agree with you is a dead end. Most of us have to do things we are not a hundred percent happy with in order to preserve relationships or keep our jobs. We all live realistic lives in which we don't always have it our way. Parents too can live with and adapt to some limits and guidelines that they don't necessarily like. If in the end these limits and guidelines improve the time they spend with you and the quality of the exchanges that you have as a couple, their adaptation will seem well worth it to them and to you. So remember, *adaptation* rather than *total agreement* is your goal as you diplomatically use the power inherent in your marriage.

The Marriage Sampler

"A successful marriage is an edifice that must be rebuilt every day."
Andre Maurois[16]

Parental influence spans the life of a couple's marriage from the earliest days until the bitter end. There is no way around it, and the only real choice left to couples is to meet this inevitable influence with grace, dignity, and respect. The Marriage Sampler will take a look at specific vignettes that will illuminate the marital issues inherent in the *Early, Middle,* and *Later* years of marriage and how they are affected by parental influence.

The Early Years are loosely defined as the period beginning with a couple's engagement and spanning the time during which a couple most appropriately struggles for autonomy, renegotiates their attachments and allegiances, and comes to consensus about their beliefs and goals as a couple. Commonly, though not exclusively, this time predates the arrival of children. Parental influence on the Early Years of a marriage is substantial and at times overwhelming for a couple. Consequently, close attention must be paid. One young woman describes just how early that influence can be felt.

> "My husband's mother pointedly described to me how as a small child, whenever my husband drew a picture of what his home would look like when he was a grown man, he always included an extension on the house for his mother and father to live in. His mother always laughed and said what a good boy he was to think of his parents that way. Still a good boy and true to those early beginnings, my husband finds it unthinkable to have a marriage with just the two of us. He still thinks his parents are going to come live with us when they get really old."

In the Early Years, subtle and not so subtle influences are brought to bear on young couples and must be addressed by them if they are to begin their marital life on firm ground.

The beginning and end of any race are the most exciting parts. We hardly pay attention to the middle because our eyes are so riveted on the finish line. But it is in the middle of the race where all the sustained hard work is going on that will enable the athlete to prevail. Much the same dynamic happens in marriage. Short shrift is given to the *Middle Years*. In our society, few people know how to handle them. What springs to mind is the drudgery, the work, a lackluster period without drama. Many marriages falter during these years as a seemingly unending and unchanging landscape stretches out before them. During this stage in a marriage, couples master the mechanics of living. Careers are often on track. Children are inevitably outgrowing their shoes, their rooms, and their families. The couple's place in their community is often secure, and they have an identity established. Despite this maturation process within the couple, their parents remain an abiding influence. The added dimension of another generation brings renewed depth to the extended family—to its meaning, to its role, and to its inherent struggles. The birth of children and their rise through the family ranks ignites "grand" parental involvement in a marriage. Though a couple may have learned successfully how to guide their parents' benevolent and confounding influences in the Early Years, their parents now may suddenly feel renewed license to be involved, and new pressures are brought to bear on a marriage.

The Middle Years generally encompass the time during which a couple raises children, begins the delicate process of including grandparents into the family, establishes careers, traverses the tricky terrain of divorce and reconstituted families, and manages their aging parents.

The Later Years are the period when a couple begins to come to terms with their own aging, the limits of their own existence, and the potential increased dependency of their already aged parents. This is a time of high anticipation in a marriage. For many, this time is invested with imagery and mythology. Retirement may loom before a couple, and within that word may lie many hopes and dreams. Rocking quietly on the porch of their home, long walks together as the sun begins to set, or traveling the world as two free spirits are just some of the portraits painted by couples as they envision their Later Years together. For others, expectations run in another direction; the Later Years may represent a narrowing of their hopes and aspirations. Fixed incomes, illness, and concerns about mortality are the themes in this chapter of their marital book. Couples' collective or disparate fantasies about their Later Years together vary widely, but generally there is a recurring theme among a majority of these couples: They often find themselves suddenly cast as caretakers of aged parents. As if it isn't hard enough to enter this stage of a marriage and keep the relationship vital and alive, couples more and more find themselves grappling with their parents' influence on their marriage in new and still potent ways.

Couples who cope with the issue of caring for aging parents need to call upon those skills they have been utilizing all along: communication, consensus, the "Royal We," and the judicious use of marital power. Along with these skills now must come a true exercise in the meaning of family. Though parents age, become infirm, and even die, their influence remains potent. Their needs may become great. With the realization of the dignity and respect due their own parents and with the wish to be treated similarly as they "age up" into these same life changes, a couple can enter this new stage in their parental relationship with a greater acceptance of the inherent need to complete the circle of family helping family. Indeed, the premise of this book is that through meeting the obligations and enjoying the benefits of family, a couple enhances their place in the world, their sense of belonging, and ultimately their sense of "We-ness." To achieve this, a couple must enter this new phase with a generosity of spirit, an acceptance of family obligations, and an ability to exercise compassion.

The Marriage Sampler will look at specific situations common to each of these three stages in a marriage, and show how the skills learned earlier in this book will serve a couple well as they journey through the years and learn to understand and cope with their parents' broad influence upon them.

CHAPTER SEVEN

Dollars and Common Sense

Money can be used in families as a vehicle for great generosity or Machiavellian-like manipulation. Socioeconomic status and family history determine a family's attitudes about money and their expectations of its use and power. For some, money is simply a commodity to be given away freely and used for enjoyment. For others, it is something to be husbanded, to be protected and nurtured, to be hoarded for a rainy day. For many families it represents security, for others love or power. For still others it holds no particular significance except as a means of putting food on the table and clothing the family. Couples rarely take a close look at the meaning of money in their families, and are consequently caught short when they face a situation in which they have to deal with money issues with their parents or each other. If their families have significantly different ways of viewing money, a couple may find themselves playing out those differences in their own marriage. Conflict will arise if they don't develop their own attitude toward money that is unique to their relationship.

The Early Years

Lillian reported this situation about three months into her marriage to Brad:

> "It took us a few months after we married to open a joint checking and savings account. My husband came home one day and handed me $100 and said, 'That's it for the week.' I was a bit put off, but didn't really know why until he asked me for my ATM bank card to keep in the drawer of his dresser. 'I'll give you money every week; you won't need it,' he said. Well, I finally got it! He thought *he* was going to give *me* an *allowance* every week and I wasn't going to have access to any of our money! He had another thing coming! I told him I would just open my own account and keep my money in it if he was going to be so difficult!"

The bell rang, and they were at it. Round One found them heatedly arguing. Lillian was outraged and couldn't believe her husband's chauvinistic behavior. Brad had always expected to give her an allowance, and it was a generous one. He couldn't figure out why she was so put out; he knew that the money was *theirs*. Round Two had Brad revealing that his own father had done this and had prided himself on "never saying no. If my mother wanted something, she got it." Lillian said that this was a feudal system. In her family, her mother managed the money, and even though her mother never earned her own money, she had equal access to everything that was theirs.

This couple needs to consult the Marriage Mirror. For Brad's family, money was a symbol of masculinity, power, and the ability of the men to take care of the women. For

Lillian's, money had been a source of equality in her parents' marriage. The task at hand for this young couple was to reconcile their differing attitudes about marital money and define the role it would play in their lives.

When they got down to a quiet discussion, they were able to *reframe* their own motivations. Lillian could see that family history motivated Brad, and that his own wish to take care of her was very strong. Brad could see that Lillian might find the system strange, first because she came from a family that functioned differently around money, and second because she earned a good salary herself. They had to compromise, but where? They finally came to a consensus that Brad needed to feel he was always taking care of her and Lillian needed to feel equal. It is hard to imagine a middle ground, but there was one for this couple. Brad gave Lillian back her bank card so she could have her own access to their money. They did, however, work out a budget and agreed that each should not take out more than that designated amount without discussing it with the other. With a bow to Brad's needs, Lillian agreed to ask Brad how he would feel if she, say, wanted to buy an expensive new dress. This simple request would give him the opportunity to say yes, just as his father had done before him. Each felt that their needs were met. Brad felt he could be generous outside the confines of their budget, and Lillian felt that she had access and autonomy in the marriage. Most important, they had short-circuited the arguments and discord that can arise when partners bring incompatible views on money matters to the marriage. Knowing your family history concerning money is necessary if you are going to be able to "mint" your own attitudes toward money.

Money Talks . . . But Keep Quiet!

Here's an invaluable piece of advice for young couples: Know when to keep quiet about financial issues when speaking to parents. Many couples find that their spending style differs from that of their parents. New purchases might elicit unsupportive or guilt-provoking remarks. Discussion about the pension plan at work that you have recently selected might elicit questions, advice, and an annoying feeling that your parents lack trust in your judgment. Taking out money for a vacation while you are still saving to buy a house might turn your parents into a cyclone of criticism. Attempts aimed at getting your parents to understand and agree with your financial lifestyle will not necessarily be possible. Therefore it is futile to engage them in too much discussion about how, why, and where you are spending your money. If your parents don't have specific information about how much money you make, save, or spend, then you are likely to avoid unnecessary conflict.

The Middle Years

During these years, the pressures of providing for children, whether it be for school tuition, clothing, or extracurricular activities, can put financial burdens on couples. Being able to finance your children's educational or career future is not as easy as it once was. A couple's parents will sometimes offer much-needed aid, but it often comes with a web of purse strings attached. The influence they expect to exert once they open that purse can vary from parent to parent. The influence a couple will allow their parents to exert will also vary. The balance between financial aid and emotional independence is a delicate one. This very issue is one that Terry, a 45-year-old architect, and his wife, Trish, had to deal with. It is typical of the money issues encountered in the Middle Years of marriage.

"My company has suffered some reversals these last few years, just when we were getting ready to send our oldest to college. I scraped together enough for half the tuition at a decent college, and though my son would probably not be going to his first choice, these schools were in the range of what we could afford. I had to go to my father-in-law to ask for help with the other half of the tuition. He had often said that education was paramount, and that if we ever needed any help just to come to him. I took him at his word and went to him with my request. Suddenly, he had a lot to say about where my son should go to school. He said he would loan us half the tuition with no interest on repayment, if we applied to his alma mater . . . which by the way was *well* out of my price range. We haggled some, and in the end, I heard him say, 'My money, my alma mater!' "

Terry was in a terrible spot. Not only did he have to humble himself to ask for the help necessary to send his child to school, but suddenly he was paying exorbitant "interest"—he had to agree to his father-in-law's terms in order to get the money. This is not an uncommon situation. Terry went home to Trish and blew his stack. He couldn't believe that after all these years of his father-in-law dangling his generosity in front of them, the moment they decided to take him up on it, they found a trap had been sprung on their outstretched hands. Terry immediately informed his wife that she needed to go and speak to her father about this, she needed to "straighten him out." His next thought was that they should forget the whole thing and their child would just have to make do with whatever they could provide for him. This thought was followed by Terry exclaiming that he was never going to speak to his father-in-law again. Trish watched as the dust flew and the words poured from her husband. She had to admit to herself that she was pretty astounded by her father's manipulation. However, she didn't speak; she just listened.

Just Listening
This is a resourceful and simple response to the situation. Terry is so angry and distraught at this moment that they

would have been destined to argue unproductively if she had engaged him in conversation. Listening gives Trish time to think about how *she* really feels about her father's rather heavy-handed conditions, as well as her husband's response to them. This technique is useful in most volatile situations.

Trish wisely suggested that she and Terry hold a plenary meeting after dinner in the den over their coffee and pie. She was buying time to think and allow her husband to cool off. It can be enormously helpful to allow time to pass between the anger-provoking event and the discussion. Couples often want to jump into the frying pan right in the heat of their initial rage and frustration, but by doing so, they end up scorched and often little is accomplished.

While sipping coffee and eating Trish's famous strawberry rhubarb pie, they got down to brass tacks. They had to reach a consensus about what to do, but first each had to find out where the other stood. Terry was still a bit hot under the collar and said he regretted asking for the money and didn't want to use any of it. Trish felt that her father's request was manipulative, but she could see his point. His alma mater was a good school, and if he was going to spend his money, he wanted to have a say. Terry countered with the assertion that money should be given without stipulations. By asking them to apply to his alma mater, his father-in-law was increasing the amount of money he *and* they would have to pitch in. This showed a disregard for the limits of their resources. The thought occurred to Terry that maybe this was his father-in-law's way of getting off the hook. If they couldn't afford such an expensive place, then they wouldn't be able to take his money at all. The question arose whether or not Trish's father really wanted to be in a position to share his money, or if he was making it impossible for them to benefit from his seeming largesse.

One thing that Terry and Trish *could* agree on was that they were not in a position to kick in any more money than they had originally stated. They were also able to agree that the lure of having their son go to a better school was great, though that would mean Trish's father had to be willing to put in more than half of the tuition, and they would be in hock for years paying him back. They talked and talked, yet ended the evening undecided. They had spent the time trying to reconcile their own needs with the demands of Trish's dad and, in the process, they had tied themselves up in emotional knots. Couples often assume that their parents' stance is set in cement. They never consider that there is room for either negotiation or movement. Often if a couple is willing to take the risk and *hold their ground*, they will see remarkable shifting taking place. Here's how Trish and Terry managed:

They finally agreed that they were not able to spend more money on tuition, that they did not want Trish's dad paying more than half, and that if he was unable to respect that and be a bit more flexible about the choice of schools, they would have to forego his money. No longer were they going to contort their own values to meet Trish's father's. Terry, not Trish, presented this to his father-in-law. It was agreed that since Terry had opened the issue, it would be wise for him to finish it up.

Terry began by thanking his father-in-law for his generous offer. (Here he was attributing the best possible motives to his father-in-law.) He said that few grandparents are able and willing to make such offers. He went on to explain how it was important for him and Trish to spend only a certain amount each year on their son's education, and so it would be impossible for them to have him apply to schools that were out of their financial range. He thanked him again, but said he could not accept his offer for help because it would strap them financially. He said no more and watched silently while his father-in-law huffed and puffed for a bit and then said that he would have to think it over. Days passed without a word, leaving Terry and Trish to surmise that her father really wanted control more than he wanted to lend them the money. However, about a week later Trish's dad phoned them. He agreed to lend them what they needed in the way in which they felt comfortable. What had happened? It turned out that by placing the ball in Trish's father's court, it had forced *him* to be the one to adapt to *their* set of requirements. This of course was only possible because Trish and Terry understood the bottom line. They knew that they were taking the risk of losing her father's aid entirely. They were willing to accept that, and so holding their ground and waiting to see if he would shift his position was not difficult.

The next step for Trish and Terry was to make an actual financial agreement with her father. Here is where couples frequently make a fatal mistake. They assume that between family members, a simple verbal agreement will suffice. Nothing could be farther from the truth. The significance and nature of family relationships makes it *particularly* important that any financial deal be made with a written agreement to back it up. This formalizing of the agreement paves the way for smoother relationships and avoids the pitfalls of resentment that can easily plague the exchanging of money in a family. Making a clear and formal agreement that encompasses a payment schedule, both for Trish and Terry (how and when they would repay the loan) and for Trish's dad (when he will make the tuition money available), leaves no questions unanswered and no doubts about how each party will behave. Then if a problem comes up, the agreement can be referred to. Learning to stick to businesslike arrangements gives the message that as *adults*, you expect to be responsible to your parents, and as *adults*, you expect your parents to be responsible to you.

The Later Years

Couples are never too old to feel their parents' influence on money matters. Whether it is a deliberate action taken by parents to influence or whether it is just the consequence of parents aging and being part of your family, powerful emotions arise in couples who are dealing with money matters at this stage in their lives. Al, a 63-year-old building contractor, spoke of his money dilemma this way:

"My wife and I have always managed okay. She is about to retire from her job as a secretary, and my kids are buying me out of my contracting business. My wife feels that now is our chance to travel, to spend our money seeing the world. Talk about a crazy plan! I'm a homebody. Seen everything I need to see. Anyway, we might need that money soon. My mother is frail, 86, and I don't think she will be able to live alone much longer. I guess I've always figured we would use that money to add on a little apartment for her and get an aide in to help out with her care. Every time my wife and I come back from visiting my mother, we have a terrible row."

Al wasn't wrong. His wife, Renee, and his mother had gotten along just fine all these years—just fine until Al's plans for his mother interfered with Renee's dreams of how they were going to spend their money and time in their later years. Arguments between them were unrelenting. Everything and everyone was thrown into the angry soup. Soon Renee was disparaging Al's sister and brother for not helping enough with his mother. Al countered that during all these years his mother had treated *her* just like a daughter, maybe even better. None of what they were saying was untrue. They just could not get themselves to communicate in a constructive manner, and they found themselves at an impasse.

Money has a different meaning and value to couples in their later years of marriage. It is usually finite in its amount, it is usually hard won and hard saved, and it has attached to it the final dreams and aspirations of the couple. For Renee, the money held many meanings, all of which she had not really conveyed to Al. She imagined using it on a vacation that would renew their relationship, long neglected during years of child-rearing and work. She dreamed of seeing foreign places and meeting people with whom she could reinvent herself and not just be Renee the housewife, secretary, and mother.

For Al, the money also held a great deal of meaning. He had worked hard and built his company up to the point that not only was it making him a good living, but was healthy enough to sell off to his boys. This gave him a great sense of satisfaction. He always got his greatest pleasure out of providing, whether it was for Renee, the boys, or his mother. His dreams didn't take him as far away as Europe or the Orient. His dreams lay harbored in everything he had worked for.

These partners need to develop an appreciation for each other's position about their money. Next they must think about where their marital allegiance lies, something they had not done in many years. Finally, they urgently must decide how to make marital sacrifices without sacrificing their marriage.

Calmly, with an emphasis on listening, they discussed their dreams with each other. With the act of listening almost always comes the opportunity to reframe what your spouse is trying to say. For instance, Renee was really hoping after all these years to rekindle her relationship with Al. If he listens to this carefully, he could be very flattered that his wife of 36 years still wants to make the effort. Her wish to do this in exotic locales should be appreciated, not discounted. For many years Renee has lived her life by the rules, done what was necessary to raise her family and keep it going. Now and at last, she wants a bit of the freedom that has been so elusive for so many years.

Al, for his part, has noble aspirations as well. His strong sense of family has brought wonderful benefits to their marriage. He has provided, been able to create a world of work for his sons, and has been there for his mother in ways that Renee must admit she respects. So, how do you meld the dreams of one spouse with the strong sense of obligation of the other?

You remain focused on the "we" of marriage. This is not a win/lose situation. Some compromise must be found. If true respect is given to the needs of each spouse, than compromise is not as daunting. As in any stage of marriage, when situations change, couples must assess how their pledge of allegiance is faring. Do they need to realign themselves? Are they really putting their marriage first? For couples like Al and Renee, years have gone by during which they paid little attention to their allegiance, years in which it seemed wholly consumed by the raising of the children and earning a living. This is a common situation. For the first time, they were really having to look at aligning themselves on the side of their marriage and its needs while remaining clearly committed to meeting their family obligations. But Al and Renee can find help in an area that is often overlooked.

The Sibling Coalition

Often after years of taking on family obligation alone, a couple loses sight of the fact that they might have siblings who also share (if not in full measure) the compelling demands of family. It was in this arena that Al and Renee found the answer to their dilemma. As Renee shouted for the twentieth time that his brother and sister don't do enough, Al realized that in fact this was true. Maybe now was the time to call in his markers. A plan was hatched that satisfied the needs of the couple while dealing with their money and relationship issues. They agreed to build on the apartment for Al's mother (who, after all was said and done, was much beloved by Renee). Also, Al's brother and sister were asked to meet some of the financial and physical obligations of taking care of her. If Al's siblings pitched in financially, Al and Renee could afford to travel. Twice a year, for four to five weeks each time, Al and Renee would take vacations to all the places that Renee had dreamed about.

During those weeks his siblings would alternate responsibility for daily visits to their mother to keep an eye on the home care situation. Much to Al and Renee's surprise, his siblings were pleased to finally have a chance to participate. Up until now they had felt that Al controlled the show and that he didn't want or need their help. As is often the case, Al the provider had not noticed how his own need to sustain everyone had cut his siblings out of the picture.

The only way this couple was able to resolve their compelling monetary and familial dilemma was to give full weight and credence to each other's needs. By repledging their allegiance to one another, they were able to find a compromise that met their family obligations while not breaking their marital backs. And they had the added benefit of being able to get help from outside their marriage to make their plan workable.

It is true that money makes the world go around, and it is equally true that it can drive couples around the bend. Diffusing the negative power of money in a marriage involves learning how money was put to use, how it was emphasized, and how having money or the lack of it was perceived by each of the partner's families. Only after doing this can a couple come to a true consensus about how they will be viewing, using, and enjoying their money in their own marriage. No matter what money dilemma a couple encounters, they must start there. Acknowledging their differences and reframing approaches to money is the next step. If you see yourself as being on the same team as your spouse, then you are sure to find a position of compromise. It is never too late in a marriage to learn this lesson and make money work for your marriage rather than against it.

CHAPTER EIGHT

There *Are* Six in the Bed

How many people have you heard insist that they were hatched from an egg, brought by the stork or simply conceived immaculately? Few people can imagine their parents engaged in wild, raucous sex. Few can imagine *much* in the way of their parents' sexuality. Although many people see their parents as nonsexual, they carry into their own marriages a vision of marital sexuality that was handed down to them when they weren't looking. Parents become a standard from which to react. In our own marriages we tend to echo or blatantly reject our parents' vision of marital sexuality. Whether a couple engages in premarital sex, adventurous sex, or seemingly run-of-the-mill sex, the level of "interference" caused by the ingrained values handed down by their parents varies. However, this interference is always there and must be heeded. No matter how independent, adult, or aged you are, there are always six in the bed come nightfall.

These influential messages are not necessarily sent in a

heavy-handed manner. They can be sent in subtle ways. Do you remember watching your mother shrug off with annoyance your father's small peck on the cheek while she was cooking dinner? Do you remember being privy to lots of affectionate hugging and kissing between your parents as you grew up? Do you remember hearing one or both of your parents make disparaging remarks about other couples and their behavior? Or do you have the burdensome memory of one parent bending your ear with inappropriate complaints about the other parent's sexual appetite or behavior? No matter how you received these sexual messages, you take them and integrate them into your own relationship. Your development as a sexual being is based upon the influences you gathered as you went along.

One couple described an interchange that took place at night after an intense argument. The wife describes herself telling her husband to go sleep somewhere else and throwing a pillow and blanket at him. He responded by yelling, "I'll be damned if I'm sleeping anywhere but in my own bed in my own house. The day we start sleeping in separate places, we can forget this marriage!"

This response was completely understandable after a look in the Marriage Mirror revealed that his parents had slept in separate rooms and had a perpetually distant marriage for as long as he could remember. Indeed, it appeared his parents had not been sexually active with each other since all of the children were quite young. Consequently, he had a definite idea of what marital sexuality was supposed to be— *the exact opposite of his parents' arrangement!*

With all of this history brought to bear on your marriage, there is every possibility that at some time the unspoken influence of your parents will affect your sexual life. A discussion with your spouse will be necessary to straighten things out, but this is more easily said than done. "Shy," "embarrassed," and "uncomfortable" are words that couples use to describe how they feel when they must talk about sexual issues with their spouse. Despite the intense level of day-to-day intimacy in most marriages, sex is often the most difficult topic to discuss. These discussions can be doubly difficult if you come from a family that felt sexual talk of any kind was taboo. In some marriages, spouses feel that if their partners really loved them, they should "know" how they are feeling. Some people wait a lifetime hoping that their spouse will figure out what the problem really is. Your own courage and encouragement from your spouse can help to make these discussions easier.

The Early Years

Noelle, a young wife, reported that if there happened to be a picture of their parents in the room when she and her husband, Bill, made love, he would have to interrupt their passion to get up and turn it face down! This behavior perplexed her, because whenever they had to stay overnight at one of their parents' homes, her husband seemed to develop an inordinate sexual appetite. The fact that his or her parents were in the next room seemed to have no effect on him, or did it?

"I don't know what to do. I just can't make love with my parents in the next room, and Bill seems to think that the situation is an aphrodisiac! We end up arguing in whispers so they won't hear us. He can't see my point of view, but I don't see why not. He can't make love at home where the picture of his folks is on a table right by the sofa in the living room! I just don't like acting flagrantly sexy in front of my folks. It makes them uncomfortable."

The young husband described above is showing a fairly common reaction to parental influence. The contradiction between his self-consciousness before a picture and his audacious sexual behavior in the homes of their parents illustrates two of the ways that parents have a kind of unconscious jurisdiction on a couple's sexual life. The very act of turning his parents' picture while making love to his wife perhaps indicates that he has a fear that they will "see" him in the act. Yet Bill's bold sexual behavior with parents in the next room demonstrates the same concern, only in reverse. Here he "dares" them to "catch him." This rebellious approach is also born of the adolescent boy in him who has not forged his own sexual system, but rather is still reacting to his parents' system.

After Noelle and Bill took a quick look in the Marriage Mirror, it was clear that Bill's parents had placed tight strictures on his behavior at home. He and his siblings were never allowed any parties once they hit adolescence, and Bill clearly remembers his parents keeping him home from some when they thought they would be "necking" parties. Bill was still trying to exercise his adolescent autonomy, in the homes of their parents.

Noelle's glance into the Mirror found a youngster whose parents delayed their acceptance of their daughter's approaching adolescence and sexual feelings for as long as they could. Her mother dressed her in childish clothing even though she begged to be allowed to wear what the other kids wore. Her father wouldn't allow her out on any dates till she was 17. And her mother had always had difficulty talking about sex with her. Even after she married, Noelle was still a little girl in her parents' eyes. She still feels like a child in the home of her parents and consequently can't entertain any adult acts of sexual behavior when she's there, even mild and open affection. Both of these young people are still acting like teenagers rather than as a couple with appropriate and acceptable sexual appetites.

Forging a mutually satisfying sexual relationship requires sifting through the subtly preprogrammed notions received from one's parents and deciding which of these you agree with and which you don't. It also requires making the shift from teen to adult so that you accept your own healthy marital sexual relationship.

A young man reports that he was raised in an Orthodox Jewish home. As he grew up, he grew away from the Orthodoxy that his parents followed. Many good things remained from the years of their influence. He had a strong sense of family and loyalty. He was a committed person. However, his upbringing was causing a problem with his wife. It seems that he could only have sex with her on Saturdays. The teachings of the religion that he had long ago set aside and the example set by his parents left him with a rigid and formal approach to his lovemaking with his young wife. His parents only had sex on Saturdays. It was considered a "mitzvah," or a blessing. This was of course sanctioned by their religion and was a joy rather than a conflict for them. His wife reported it this way:

> "Saturday . . . I have things to do on Saturday. Cleaning and food shopping for the next week. Also, though I love to have sex with Seth, frankly I would just thrill to a bit more spontaneity from him. He's a good lover, but he can't do it any other day. He says it's because he's so tired during the week from work. Okay, I'll buy that, but whatever happened to Sunday?"

Seth was, as we all are, a product of his parents' sexual approach to marriage. It was natural that sex on Saturdays, a blessing and part of religious law, was part of their routine. For them it posed no conflict and no dilemma because it was backed by their faith. For Seth, sex on Saturday represented an unconscious integration of what he had witnessed while growing up. A quick look into the Marriage Mirror would have confirmed this for him.

Seth and his wife were about to enter into an area of increasing dissatisfaction and conflict if they didn't take the time to respect their differences and come to a compromise that was comfortable for each of them. With the help of a counselor, they were able to see how the differences in the ways they were brought up determined how they dealt with sexual issues. Seth's wife had come from a family that had some measure of sexual profligacy in its history. Her father had had a number of affairs during his marriage to her mother. Seth's wife was determined to have a faithful marriage, and part of the reason she was so drawn to Seth was that he was so loyal, steady, and predictable. Now, all that predictability was driving her nuts. Seth, for his part, was drawn to his wife's open emotions, common sense, and ability to see things for what they were without having to rely on "teachings" to guide her.

The work they were doing, which is always a necessary first step in these situations, involved taking an honest look at the preprogramming that came from their families and seeing if it works for them in their own sexual system. They addressed the guilt Seth might feel from having sex on days other than Saturday. He was able to realize that unknowingly he was trying to avoid risking any more "disapproval" from his parents such as he experienced when he gave up the Orthodox lifestyle. Consequently he was unconsciously a "good boy" and playing by the rules—in this area, anyway. They addressed the need for his wife to be sensitive to these unconscious rules. Seth had to recognize the frustration his wife was experiencing at not being able to express herself sexually at any time other than when he "allowed it." He was asked to recognize the appropriateness of her requests and the rejection she experienced when her sexual advances were constantly rebuffed.

Forming a new sexual structure in their marriage was not going to be easy. It felt forced and a little uncomfortable when the counselor suggested that they not only have sex on Saturday, but that they have sex one other day during the week, on a night chosen by Seth's wife. Both agreed to it, but it was startling to them how much resistance they *both* experienced on that other day. On close scrutiny, they realized that Seth felt guilty and his wife felt wanton, as if she were doing something wrong. They were able to integrate the absurdity as well as the seriousness of the situation into their discussion of their sexual needs. They gave each other humorous names. Seth was the "mitzvah maker" and his wife was "sexy Sadie." These names gave broad acknowledgment to their histories as well as to the feelings they were both experiencing. It also gave them a humorous handle to hold onto so that when they talked, they could remember not to take everything so seriously. Over time, they were able to broaden their sexual life and repertoire to make it their own, and not just a reflection of their past.

The Middle Years

Cal and Debra, a couple in their early fifties, were smack dab in the Middle Years of their marriage. It was a time characterized by teenage children, seemingly thousands of extracurricular commitments, job pressures, and money constraints. To add to the pressure, they had just seen Cal's mother through the awful period after the death of Cal's dad from cancer. His mother had fallen apart, leaving Cal and Debra, as well as Cal's sister Helen, to pick up the pieces. Two years of constant phone calls, weekends of driving his mother to go shopping and to the hairdresser, and coping with her general depression. On top of it all, Cal was dealing with his own feelings of loss and the sense of his own mortality that often accompanies the death of a parent. Cal and Debra characterized their marriage as dull, "just existing." They had little time together. Conversations resembled strategic planning sessions for military incursions. They were juggling the lives of their three children and Cal's mother, as well as their own. Their time together was spent paying bills and hemming prom dresses in front of the TV late into the night. Sex was a fleeting thought that never went beyond the planning stage. They were facing many of the issues that couples in their Middle Years face; feeling many of the same vague twinges of regret over neglected marital "we-ness" and the lusty sexual time they had once spent together. Suddenly something happened that woke them up and rattled them.

Quite uncharacteristically, Cal's mother decided to join some of her friends for a weekend in the Poconos for widows and widowers. After they got over the shock at hearing the news, they were pleased that she was going away, and quite honestly saw it as free time to get some of their own chores done. During the weekend, Cal's mother met a lovely man who had been widowed for about the same length of time that she had. They struck up a friendship and began seeing each other to go to the movies or out to dinner. At first these contacts were occasional, and they didn't affect the amount of attention that Cal and Debra had to pay to their mother, but her mood was better and she spent more time talking about things she was going to do. Then suddenly the relationship intensified, and Cal's mother announced that she and her friend Byron were going away on a cruise together. His mother was excited, even titillated. She chirped on and on about what she was going to wear, see, and do on the trip.

When she revealed that she and Byron were sharing a stateroom on the boat, Cal was thrown for a loop. His mother was experiencing a sexual renaissance. She was wearing makeup and a slightly higher heel. She was going to the hairdresser *twice* week, and some of the dresses she purchased to take on the cruise were downright sexy.

Suddenly Cal had mixed feelings. He was happy that his mother was finally out of her depression. Though he hated to see his father replaced in his mother's heart, he also had witnessed her suffering, and he knew that this was right. Anyway, Byron was a very nice man and treated his mother well. But this sexual thing was too much. She had never been this overtly sexual when his father was alive. She held hands with Byron and kissed him in front of them. With disgust and a good measure of jealousy, Cal made disapproving noises about them to Debra. He had even received a phone call from Byron's daughter expressing her concern that their parents were rushing into something like two kids would do.

Cal wasn't jealous of Byron taking over his role with his mother, he was grateful for the relief! His discomfort arose from the fact that he had never really considered his parents as sexual people, and consequently he was startled to find his mother so actively enjoying this new status. Had she gone crazy?

Most of us never get to see our parents in the heyday of their sexual life. By the time we are conscious of them as sexual people, they are in the Middle Years of their marriage and are often not as overtly sexual with one another as they might have been had we caught a glimpse of them in the Early Years of their marriage. To Cal, his mother and father, though loving, had never appeared very sexual. (It is most common for children to deny their parents as sexual people when they reach their own adolescence, because it is too frightening to imagine one's parents experiencing the same hormonal hell raising that they are going through.) Suddenly his mom was saying things to them like, "You two should get out more, you never seem to have any fun."

Soon he found himself angry at his wife, without consciously knowing why. He started blaming her for never having time for him and always putting the children first. She was working hard and doing her part; she couldn't understand why all of a sudden she was getting mercilessly needled about how she looked and how she dressed. She started to feel inadequate and unappealing. She began to wonder if he was having an affair and was constantly comparing her to some mystery woman.

The arguing escalated until Debra, in a complete state of frustration and worry, called a meeting. Once they began to talk, it became clear that there was no mystery woman, nor were they really so far apart in their desires for their marriage. Both had wished, for a long time, that they had paid more attention to the romantic side of their life together. They had had talks about their lack of time alone together many times in the past. But never before had Cal been attacking and critical of Debra. Never before had his words had such vehemence. When asked why he was so angry and accusing, he blurted out, "I'm tired of watching my mother having the time of her life while I spend the best years of mine withering away." There it was—he was jealous because his mother was having the sex life that he wanted with Debra but that long ago had drowned in the day-to-day Middle Years of their marriage. His mother was having the excitement and fun he longed for.

Can sexual pressure from parents be brought to bear on a marriage in its Middle Years? Clearly the answer is yes. In this case, the pressure of Cal's mother's newfound sexuality heightened his disappointment in his own lack of sexual activity. The shock of recognizing that his mother, some 30 years his senior, had a better sex life was almost too much to take. To that end, the pressure this change in his mother's status wrought on his own marriage was quite positive. Although the strain and initial lack of communication were difficult, Cal and Debra realized that they both wanted the same thing. They both wanted to feel again the romance and excitement they had once felt for each other. They quickly booked a four-day weekend at a romantic inn. They threw aside their daily commitments and just decided to go. Cal's mother was not the only one who was going to experience a sexual renaissance if they could help it! Though they were still bogged down in the day-to-day drudgery of their lives, that weekend alone made them realize that they could still have an active and exciting sex life together. They built into their schedule four such weekends a year and took the time to reconnect with each other.

The Later Years

Fay, a woman of 64, reported astonishment at the influence her aged mother-in-law was having on her sex life. She and her husband had most recently been thrust into the role of caregivers to his aging mother.

"My husband and I have always enjoyed sex, though I guess we never had it day and night! But after the kids finally all moved out, we were beginning to feel a new freedom. Well, three months ago my husband's mother came to live with us. She has trouble sleeping and will often get up at night. Every time my husband wants to have sex, I find myself listening intently for her footsteps in the hall, rather than enjoying myself. She has been known to open our door unexpectedly when she wanders around at night. Jack gets annoyed with me because I can't seem to get myself comfortable enough to take pleasure from sex. He keeps telling me to simply forget that she's in the house . . . but I can't!"

Fay and Jack find themselves with a job that more and more couples in their later years are filling. They have become the caregivers to one of their parents. They had thought of many things when they imagined the pressures of having Jack's mother come live with them . . . but they never divined that their sex life would be affected. Wandering into their room at night was only one of the ways that her presence put the brakes on their sex life. Also a factor were all the subtle signs of her attitude about affection and sex that were slowly and imperceptibly being felt, especially by Fay.

Jack's mother came from a different generation. Displays of affection and outward exhibition of sexual behavior were unthinkable. Fay found herself subtly altering her affectionate and sexual behavior toward her husband despite the fact that she was in her own home and a grown woman. If Jack pinched her behind or gave her a hug in front of her mother-in-law, Fay reported feeling "her eyes boring into me as if I was a teenager leading her little boy astray!" Jack, on the other hand, seemed not to notice his mother's "disapproving" glance, as Fay put it, and he offered the unproductive advice that she should "just forget about Mom."

A number of issues were at hand that caused the conflict between Fay and Jack.

1. They had *differing roles* as the caretakers of Jack's mother and consequently differing feelings of responsibility toward her.
2. They had *differing thresholds* of discomfort about being affectionate in front of Jack's mother.
3. With the presence of his mother in their house, Jack and Fay, in different ways, were reverting back to *adolescent behavior*.
4. They had not *anticipated* her attitude about sex affecting their lives.

You might wonder how their differing roles in the caretaking of Jack's mother might influence their sexual activity. Fay had to make clear to Jack that since she was the one home all day and the one looking after his mother, she felt a particular sense of responsibility for the woman's well-being. She also was the one most affected by his mother's attitudes, style, and personality. By the time Jack got home at night from his office, his mother was comfortably ensconced in front of *Wheel of Fortune* and gave him nary a glance. Fay, on the other hand, felt that her responsibility extended into the night. Her mother-in-law's wanderings not only could result in an embarrassing situation if she walked in on Jack and her making love, but they also could result in a fall or some other type of disaster. All these things preyed on Fay's mind, for she was the primary caregiver. Fay had known, when she agreed to having Jack's mother live with them, that this would be her job. She just didn't know how much that sense of responsibility would affect every aspect of her adult existence. "It's like having another child that you always have to think of first. I thought this time in my life would be for me and Jack," she said. The icing on the cake, of course, was that she was often annoyed that Jack seemed to be able to separate himself from the situation and act as if he didn't care. He expressed his take on the situation this way: "Look, if she falls at night, she falls. There is nothing we can do about it if she insists on getting up and walking around. I'm not staying up all night to worry about it. I need my sleep. And if she walks in on us while we're fooling around, that's just too bad for her. We've asked her to knock."

Clustered in those few sentences were all of Jack's attitudes toward the situation. He doesn't feel as responsible as Fay. He has a much higher threshold of guilt about expressing himself sexually in front of his mother. And he displays just a hint of the adolescent who doesn't want his life ruled by the presence of his parent. He even offers up a bit of a challenge about getting caught.

Fay was overly responsible, taking a mother's role once again. She also was not comfortable expressing herself sexually around her mother-in-law. Her feeling that she was looked upon by her mother-in-law as too sexual and someone who was corrupting Jack was a remnant of adolescent guilt over sexuality. Finally, this couple was stuck in a kind of shock state over the potent effect Jack's mother was having on their sex life. There certainly were at least *three* in the bed every night in this household.

As with any difficulty that arises from the outside pressure of a parent's behavior or attitude, a couple must examine their allegiances and see if, in fact, they are appropriately pledged to each other. In the case of Jack and Fay, they had had a major shift in their status as a family and had not really fully pledged that through the change they would keep each other close and squarely in mind.

They had rights as a couple, a fact that Fay was having trouble remembering. They had power to structure and orchestrate the influences on their marriage, another fact that Fay was losing sight of. The moment Fay heard Jack suggest that she "just forget that my mother is in the house," she should have called a meeting. Solutions were really not that hard to come by once Fay (the responsible) and Jack (the detached) opened up discussion about their situation.

They decided to use sibling connections to afford them some respite for a long weekend once a month. They put a lock on their bedroom door—something they never believed in when they had small children in the house, but times change. Finally, once the dialogue was opened up, Jack could appreciate just how much work and attention Fay was devoting to his mother. His laissez-faire attitude about Fay's concerns had left her feeling diminished and disrespected. He made an effort to spend more time with his mother and spell Fay for a few hours on the weekends. Finally, they spoke with Jack's mother about privacy and personal styles. Before this conversation, Jack and Fay discussed who would be the Speaker of the House in this situation. Fay felt too uncertain and vulnerable to do it alone, and Jack, without Fay's gentler touch, might have transformed the conversation into a confrontation between mother and "adolescent" son about his rights! In the end, they decided to do it together. Without actually having to confront her puritanical views, Jack and Fay expressed to her how important it was for them to feel comfortable in their own home. His mother of course didn't quite see what she was doing to make them uncomfortable, and the two of them didn't want to be too confrontational with her. However, the unity they felt with each other now about this issue made it possible to put up with and have a common understanding of his mother's influence.

In all these situations, resolution and change were not immediate or consistent. Couples who take the time and have the courage to talk about and implement change should be cautioned against expecting too much too soon, or expecting that once change begins that it will advance at a steady pace. Hoping that the situation will go away is never productive. Using all the resources at your disposal and looking for creative solutions will bring results.

CHAPTER NINE

The World of Work

Parental influence on a child's career choice can be felt at any point in that child's life. Career choices are influenced by everything from offhand comments to flagrant campaigning on the part of a parent. A parent's hopes and dreams for a child may come into direct conflict with the child's own inclinations and strengths. And nowadays, with the job market so tight and careers being derailed by corporate downsizing, parents have yet another opportunity to step in and influence, to help or hinder.

The way couples mesh the world of work with their marriages can be directly correlated to the way in which their parents handled that same issue. Your parents' attitudes about when, where, and how much they worked will mirror your own attitudes. Did work come in second to family life, or did work come first and outweigh all other considerations in your home? Was work and the workplace a bone of contention between your parents, or was there harmony?

Did both of your parents work, or was one of them at home to raise the children? All these questions and more should be answered by each of you as you enter into discussion of the way the world of work will be integrated into your own married life.

For Simon and Cynthia, these questions weren't addressed until well into the second year of their marriage. Simon is a freelance writer who does most of his work on his computer at home. Due to the nature of freelance work, his schedule has no particular regularity. However, once he has a job, the work is often intense, with pressing deadlines and total immersion on his part. Cynthia is the coproducer of a successful television show for children. When they met, they felt they were meant for each other. They were both creative, intelligent, and often consumed by their work. They felt able to understand each other's needs. They romanticized an existence of interesting friends and respect for each other's creative inclinations. But recently Simon and Cynthia had begun to argue. Though their creativity was the common ground and the cement of their relationship, each had his or her own idea of what constituted being successful.

Of course, the arguing wasn't initially focused on the issue of work; it was, as is often the case, deflected onto another issue. Cynthia felt that since Simon was home all day, he should take on more of the household duties. She was often short and annoyed with him when she would come home after a long day to find newspapers lying around the living room and lunch dishes in the sink. It was getting to the point where Cynthia was preparing for a fight before she even walked in the door and, frankly, Simon wasn't looking forward to his wife coming home.

Simon was finding himself increasingly annoyed with Cynthia's disregard for their time together—always opting to do just one more thing at the office, or attend an office-related function on the weekends. He felt she had become "power-hungry," which was not something he found appealing in his wife. Their arguments ended with Cynthia implying that Simon was lazy and Simon stating his distaste for his wife's ambitious, aggressive approach to work.

A look into the Marriage Mirror revealed how their parents' work attitudes had directly influenced them both. Simon saw his father's workaholic ways as a source of great tension in his family. His mother was always unhappy because she felt her husband didn't spend enough time at home or have enough of an appreciation for how hard it was for her to raise their three sons virtually on her own. Simon had always been close to his mother and sympathized with her situation. He was often her confidant and shared her anger. He had been deeply disappointed with his father for missing Little League games and father/son Scout dinners. His father's attitude toward work, and his up-close view of his mother's unhappiness, molded his ideas. Simon had vowed early on never to be that type of husband or father. Freelance work seemed the perfect solution.

Cynthia came from a family in which both her parents had important and demanding jobs. You might say that they were both "modified" workaholics. Though there was time for the family, much of it was spent in discussion of how things were progressing at work or at school. Achievement and success were nurtured and supported. In her family, the standard for success was clear and well defined, not something that was questioned. Lately, Cynthia had been hearing offhand comments from her parents about Simon's freelance status. They were concerned, and wanted him to find "steady" work—the kind they could understand and that would meet their criteria for success. Here was the problem.

Though Cynthia appreciated Simon's writing and creativity, she wasn't sure if he was going to make a success of it. She was fearful that Simon wasn't ambitious enough. The newspapers on the living room floor weren't the problem, it was Cynthia's nagging fear that Simon wasn't working hard enough to succeed. From Cynthia's value system, Simon's relaxed approach to his work looked lazy. From Simon's perspective, Cynthia's total immersion in her work reflected her lack of commitment to the marriage. He was also quietly concerned about what type of mother she was going to make once they had children. Would she be the female version of his father—never home and too busy to participate?

When they got married, they thought they knew what work meant to each of them individually and as a couple, but in truth, they each had made many assumptions and hadn't taken the time to reflect and inspect their points of view. Simon and Cynthia are facing the dilemma of defining big words such as "success," "home," and "family." With a little respect and compromise, common goals can be established. Understanding the past and integrating it into the present is the task at hand for this young couple.

The Early Years

Monica, a motivated and energetic woman of 25, is a hairstylist and has set a goal of owning her own salon. She has run into a good deal of conflict with her husband, Daniel, and describes it this way:

> "Daniel is a floor foreman for a large dairy company. He has worked for them, as has his dad, for over 15 years. He's very well liked there. When I told Dan that I wanted to open my own salon, he didn't give me the response I expected. Instead of full support, I got a lot of hesitation on his part. I was surprised and hurt, to say the least. Lately he has a lot to say about my plans. Mostly he tries to discourage me, and uses words like "dreaming" and "risky" and questions my ability to carry a whole business on my own. I don't understand it. He has always said that I'm the best hairdresser that he knows. Now I'm furious and feel that every discussion of my plans is going to end up in a huge battle. Conse-

quently, I don't bring anything up any more. I've never felt so alone in my marriage as I do now."

When asked about what he thought of Monica's ability as a hairdresser, Daniel offered nothing but praise. He even commented on the fact that her clients liked her so much that they had followed her from one salon to another over the years. When asked why this obvious talent couldn't be translated into the success of her own salon, he talked of how complex and risky it was to own your own company. After all, it would involve dealing with expenses, responsibility, and actual money management. Monica, of course, felt undermined and undervalued. She felt that if her husband couldn't back her up on her career dream, then he really didn't mean all those positive things he said about her talents. Over time lots of arguments ensued, as well as a subtle eroding of Monica's conviction. This coincided with her growing sense of dissatisfaction with Daniel.

Ah, reflections of the past superimposed on the present! One look in the Marriage Mirror disclosed their families' histories and expectations with regard to career, risk-taking, and providing. Monica's parents had run a family business together. Her father owned a tire repair and installation garage. He did fairly well at it, and over the years, with her mother's help as bookkeeper and secretary, they were able to make a decent living for the family. He had been completely at ease with the idea of working for himself. In fact, he "pitied the poor soul who was a company man." This attitude had been infused into Monica from years and years of exposure to it. Additionally, she was always told that she was like her dad in so many ways.

Daniel's family was populated with company men *and* women. *Longevity* in working for the company, as well as seeing yourself as *invaluable* to the company, were trademarks of their family work history. His dad was foreman at the dairy before him, and was rewarded for his loyalty with promotions and good will. Daniel was following closely in his father's footsteps and was seen by the company as a good investment, since his work ethic and his attitude mirrored his dad's pretty closely. His mother was a line worker at a Westinghouse plant. She too had longevity on the job. She had a good pension and benefits, as well as a feeling that her co-workers were her second family. She had, in her own mind, attained the American Dream.

Monica's drive for independence kept bumping into Daniel's need for security and his sense that he could count on her ability to make a living. This was a conundrum of sorts, since Dan knew that part of what attracted him to Monica was her self-confidence and drive, her energy and charisma. For Monica, Dan's loyalty, which mirrored what she saw between her parents, was high on her list of attractions. That was why his lack of support for her endeavor felt so much like a betrayal to her.

Few young couples think of their parental work history and attitudes as something they should attend to. However, in a very real way, those influences play a part in the course a couple's work lives will take. In the case of Daniel and Monica, those influences got played out in such a way that each member of the couple felt unsupported and misunderstood. Daniel swore that his concerns about Monica starting a business had nothing to do with his regard for her. He was telling the truth. The real motivating factor in his uneasiness was the weight of family history and lack of experience in living any other way than his family had lived all these years. Monica interpreted his resistance to her plan as an attack on her. Misunderstood and attacked for his attitude, Daniel found himself angry and disappointed in Monica. Compromise and common goals must be established. Understanding of the past and integration of it into the present is the task at hand.

Dan and Monica must find a way to allow for Monica's dream without raising Dan's anxiety level about the financial risk they are taking. Together they must look at worst-case scenarios. Exactly how much money will they lose if the salon fails? Is there a way to save money beforehand in order to ease the worry about financial stability that Dan feels so keenly? If they work on the plan for Monica's salon together, they will be able to integrate Dan's worries and Monica's dreams more easily. They will also be carrying on their families' traditions of family members working side by side.

The Middle Years

The famous author John Dos Passos wrote, "People don't choose their careers; they are engulfed by them."[17] This is never more true than in the case of entering a family business. The couple who are coping with one of their members participating in a family business is already under a unique kind of stress. All of the usual issues that a couple has to face and that can cause conflict are heightened. When sorting things out, the couple not only has to deal with their own preferences, but often with the preferences of a council of people intimately interested in every nuance of their life. For those couples who take their vows to each other *and* to the family business, an almost unimaginably dense jungle lies ahead. It is filled with traps, smothering humidity, and a lack of daylight. It can also be filled with unique beauty and breathtaking wonders.

Some families manage to traverse the inherent difficulties of melding marriage and family business successfully enough that they fall into a comfortable give-and-take arrangement. Shifts occur in the equilibrium of these arrangements when normal life changes take place. In the case of Rozalyn and Nolan, this happened when Roz's mother fell ill and her father needed to take over more of her care at home. She described this Middle Years problem this way:

"My husband entered my father's insurance business years ago when we first got married. They have built it up together, and they haven't had too many conflicts over the years. I hate when they do argue, because I always feel torn between supporting Nolan and being my father's daughter. Recently my mother has become ill and requires more support at home. I would do it, but I work full-time as a third grade teacher. My father must assume the bulk of the responsibility. This has made a big shift in the office. Nolan has been working incredibly long hours making up for my dad's absence. That was fine for a while, but now it looks like this might be a long-term problem. My father refuses to talk about it, saying that as soon as my mother regains some of her strength, he will be back in the office in full force. We understand that this company was Dad's baby, but Nolan is at the point of needing another pair of hands, or they are going to lose business and tarnish their reputation for prompt, complete service. After all, Nolan takes pride in the business's reputation as well. Nolan thinks they should hire on someone to help, Dad is stonewalling, and I feel in the middle."

Surely Nolan's suggestion to hire another competent agent was logical and reasonable. But his hands were tied because, after all these years, Roz's father still held the majority control of the company. Nolan had been thinking for years that he should discuss updating the original shareholders agreement with his father-in-law, but things were running so smoothly he just assumed that they were on a fifty-fifty footing. All of a sudden his father-in-law was using his majority holding to disregard Nolan's suggestion. This was infuriating as well as disappointing to both Nolan and Roz. They couldn't understand how after all the years of Nolan's scrupulous loyalty, he was being cast as the junior partner and his opinions were being overridden.

Roz knew that there was trouble when she alternated between feeling annoyed with her husband for expressing his frustration with her father (finding herself defending and protecting the "old man") and being angry at her dad for not being reasonable and seemingly mistrusting them after so many years of loyalty. Nolan started saying things such as "Your father better change his mind soon, or I'm going to have to think about legal alternatives." This threw Roz into a complete tailspin. Suddenly they had gone from being involved in a happy family business to being opponents in a hornets' nest of accusations and misunderstanding. Roz's arguments with Nolan escalated despite the fact that she felt that he was right. She was afraid he would approach her dad too aggressively, especially now, when he was dealing with so much at home with her sick mother.

Forced but calm conversation at a plenary meeting advanced three major issues: First, they both felt slighted and hurt by Roz's dad's attitude toward Nolan's rights and power at the office. Second, they felt very bad that he had experienced so much stress both in caring for Roz's mother and in not being able to work as he always loved to. And last, despite the shareholders' agreement written two decades ago when Nolan was just out of graduate school and starting out, Nolan had made major and comparable contributions to the growth and success of the business and by this time should have an equal say in what to do with it.

They were also able to talk about Roz's divided loyalties and her guilt in feeling that this whole situation could have been avoided if only *she* were free to take care of her mother. They were able to recognize that they were not children, nor should they be treated as such. They were able to recognize that the "Royal We" afforded them the right to determine the impact that changes in the business would have on their married life. They were able to recognize that as much as they were invested in the business, so was Roz's father, and he had always acted in the past with good sense and an equitable hand. For these reasons they decided to present Roz's dad with a royal decree. They determined that the Speaker of the House should be Nolan, but that Roz should be present. Her presence was required because the focus of what they had to discuss really revolved around the impact the shift at the office had had on their immediate family. They also decided that rather than distress Roz's mother in any way, they should have the discussion either at their house or at the office.

So what was the decree? They needed to identify the events that triggered the discussion of hiring on another agent for the business. Nolan was working too hard, was never home, and was feeling that he couldn't meet the task with his usual level of excellence. Roz and Nolan wisely decided to set aside all the other issues and focus on what would give them more immediate relief. They knew that at some point they would have to address the issue of the shareholders' agreement and equity in the company, but at this point they felt that Roz's father was dealing with enough. They met him one evening at the office, brought in sandwiches, and made a declarative statement about what they needed. They described how the current situation, which was now months old, needed to be addressed. They said that something had to be done to relieve Nolan's workload. He was never home, hadn't seen the kids for more than 50 minutes in the past month, and felt that the company's reputation had begun to suffer. They offered no solution, knowing that the last time they did that, they came up against a stone wall. Their final statement was that no matter how it was resolved, Nolan could no longer be responsible for the quality or speed with which everything at the office was expedited.

Roz's father was now in the driver's seat, though he may have felt like he was in the hot seat. It was up to him to respond to their clear appraisal with some type of solution. He immediately said that he didn't want anyone else meddling in the business, that he and Nolan could handle things themselves. Roz countered that it didn't really matter at this point if it was someone they hired or her dad, but another pair of hands had to be in the office. Roz suggested that if her father felt so strongly about not having someone else in the office, he should consider hiring someone to take care of her mother during the day. He vetoed this as well; he felt too guilty to let another person take on that role.

Seemingly boxed into another corner, Roz and Nolan simply stated that he couldn't have it both ways. Something had to give, and it was either a caregiver in the house or another agent in the office. They concluded the discussion at that point, telling him that he had to decide and that they couldn't do it for him. Similar to the example of Terry asking for college tuition from his father-in-law, Nolan and Roz had to walk away and leave the ball in Roz's dad's court. A few breathless days passed, but in the end he agreed to hire a junior associate agent to help out for the time being.

Nolan and Roz made a declarative statement about what they wanted, held their ground, and didn't mix too many issues into the pot. Over time, Nolan addressed the issue of getting his rightful share of the practice and of the decisions that affected the practice. Good will and common sense prevailed, but not without Roz's father first having to grudgingly acknowledge that Nolan was an equal. He was no longer the mentor and Nolan the student. He was giving up control of something he thought of as his own. He was confronting the change in his life with his wife. He was facing mortality. Time was going by, and that meant thinking about passing the company on after he was gone. This was a slow process, but eventually time and talk resolved the future and present issues.

Passing the mantle—this is one of the largest, often the last one, of the great stumbling blocks in the long progress of a couple coping with the labyrinth of a family business. It is often something haggled over, especially if there is more than one child up for succession. In many cases the decision is kept dangling over family members' heads as a means to keep them in line, as well as to protect the power base of the patriarch or matriarch of the company. No matter what the reason, the succession process is often an uncomfortable decision-making process, and it is sometimes postponed until there is almost no time left—frequently until a couple is in their Later Years.

The Later Years

Finally you are advancing to the years when power is yours, your confidence is intact, and you begin expecting (if you haven't been already expecting for years) to take over the helm of a business that you have considered your own for decades. All your hard work will pay off, and you will be tapped to be the next CEO or president of the family firm. Your parent or in-law is getting frail and has finally come to the conclusion that it is time to take an emeritus position when it comes to the business. Seems simple. You've been working at every level of the business for years. You know everything there is to know. You have in fact been running the business without anyone noticing. How difficult could a transition be? A few papers to sign? A nice retirement or buyout package for your parent or in-law? Just wait.

Lorraine describes this difficult scene:

"My husband has been working in my family's soap manufacturing business for 35 years. He has been the chief financial officer for a long time. My brother Mel is a vice president, and my dad is the CEO. Over the years my husband has grown close to my father . . . as close as a son. You might even say closer, since my brother often has harebrained schemes for the company that my dad and Tom have to squelch. He got them into some difficulty a few years ago by moving ahead without consulting the business. On paper his idea looked good, but it turned out to be a financial disaster. My husband had to find a way out of the agreement. It wasn't easy, but he did it. My brother is a great guy, but he doesn't exactly have the financial head for business that my husband has. He is, however, great at selling our product to other companies and stores. When Dad announced that he was going to be retiring soon, a chill went down my spine. Who was going to take over as CEO? I think that my husband simply assumed that it would be him. He seems to have had the inside track with my dad for many years. My brother and his wife must have assumed it would be Mel, because he is the natural son. However, they couldn't have been that confident, because they began a lobbying campaign to get my father to choose Mel. I was upset. I know how hard my husband has worked, and it seems to me he deserves the position. So I began my own little campaign. You must understand this is not my husband's style. I had Dad and Mom to dinner and discussed the situation, building Tom up and talking about all he had done. After my parents left, Tom lit into me. He was furious and embarrassed that I had stooped so low as to try to prompt my father to give him the job. We have been fighting ever since. I guess we are both really tense about the situation, though Tom says he is not."

Once they could stop fighting, they took a look into the Marriage Mirror. What they saw was a reminder of who they had been in their families of origin. Tom had always been a do-gooder. He had taken on the role of man of the house when his father died. He put his siblings through school and kept his mother well cared for her whole life. But Tom was quiet and never made a fuss about himself, so often his efforts went untouted, though he had always been respected. On some level he felt that the CEO position meant finally getting the acknowledgment that he had never overtly received in his life. Being tapped to take over the family business may seem like your last chance for your parent or in-law to finally endorse you, the last time that a public display of approval can be received. For that reason, this prospect can relegate even the most mature men and women to the status of children. They await parental approval and acceptance. This attitude, coupled with their own sense of having mastered the world and being experienced in their own rights, makes for a tug-of-war of feelings: "Pick me, pick me" versus "I don't need anyone to tell me I can do what I already know how to do."

When Lorraine took a look, she saw something interesting as well. She too was a good girl, while her brother Mel's antics hardly received the punishment they deserved. She had always resented that she walked the straight and narrow while he got away with so much. Lorraine felt that if Tom got tapped for the job, that would be a sort of endorsement of her and her choice of a husband. She would finally, though vicariously, get some of the approval she sought from her dad. This put Tom under a lot of pressure to "make it" for *her*. He was not the sort of person who got caught up in that kind of "childish neediness," he told her. This sparked another round of fighting in which Tom responded to additional pressure on top of what he was already feeling and Lorraine felt completely misunderstood. Certainly Lorraine wanted her father's approval, but that was only a part of why she was campaigning so hard for Tom. She also believed that he was the right man for the job.

Reframing Lorraine's attempt to curry favor on Tom's behalf revealed the most positive of intentions. What man wouldn't want a wife who believed so strongly in him that she was willing to fight for him? *Reframing* Tom's discomfort with her tactics, and his anger at her making a spectacle of herself on his behalf, revealed a man of great scruples. What woman wouldn't want a husband who had so much integrity and honesty that he just wanted his work to speak for itself?

At this point, they were able to talk more comfortably about what Lorraine's father was doing. He was allowing himself to be cornered by each camp and letting them talk. He was dragging his feet about making his choice. He was keeping both Mel and Tom dangling, leaving them uncertain about their futures. Tom and Lorraine realized that this behavior was his way of handling his own discomfort about having to make a decision. Together, they decided not to get involved in a campaign, not to get caught up with Mel and his wife in discussions about it. The final decision was something over which they had very little control. So they resolved instead to put their energy into something else. They felt that they had to face *worst-case scenarios* in order to be prepared as a couple for what might come. They talked about what to do in the event that Mel was chosen. Would Tom stay on as second in command after all these years as his father-in-law's right hand? What if he was selected, and had to deal with Mel's disappointment and resentment over not being chosen? In talking about all these eventualities, they were able to anticipate their own feelings and reactions. They were able to come to a common understanding about how they would face each possible scenario, and they were able to keep their marriage in focus as their most important asset.

In the end, Lorraine's dad decided on joint ownership and leadership. He divided tasks based on the strengths of each man. He, in fact, did the right thing. Through the experience, Lorraine and Tom learned how they could face adversity, how they could rely on each other, and how much their marriage gave them strength to carry on.

The family business is not always a place of stress and high intensity. It can be a well-defined common ground on which families meet and interact respectfully. Anticipation and preparation are watchwords. Couples must not lose sight of themselves as powerful, entitled to certain rights, and capable of setting boundaries and limits. They must remember that families rarely wish to lose members and will make many adaptive efforts to keep members in the fold. Couples must always clarify what they need so that they open discussion with other family members with a clear goal, consensus between themselves, and an unwavering sense of their right to function as a couple. The word "family" in the phrase "family business" does not have to be a harbinger of problems, but rather can denote a comfortable, open, and mutually respectful group of related people engaged in a shared endeavor.

CHAPTER TEN

Grandparents

"A home without a grandmother is like an egg
without salt."
Florence King[18]

The birth of children to a couple brings a new dimension to the term "extended family." Once children enter the picture, the true benefits of the extended family can be felt. The genuine gratification inherent in well-guided family relations has no greater place or time. For here, three generations at once can feel the warmth and nurturance of this wonderful conglomerate. It is also simultaneously true, however, that stress exponentially increases when grandchildren join the family.

If you have high-voltage, contact-hungry parents, be assured that no matter how well you have modified their behavior toward you as a couple, the birth of your child will rekindle old behaviors. There is often a renewed blurring of the boundaries and a stampede of grandparental incursions into the private realm of the new family. The birth often revives in them a wish to have a second chance at parenting. It may present a heretofore lost opportunity for them to guide you, their grown children, once more as they had done when you were young. Their opinions may flow freely, backed by an authority they say comes from having "done this before." Their need for contact can have many origins. There is of course the simple, uncomplicated fact that the joy of raising a child is so potentially delicious the second time around. Other more complex motivations might include competition with the other set of grandparents, living out unrealized opportunities (for example, finally having a girl child in the family after the birth of nine boys), or the need that may exist for the widowed or deeply unhappy grandparent to fill a void in his or her own life.

Some grandparents do not meet the profile of the border bounder. These low-voltage grandparents are often shadowy, distant figures who are set apart from the grandchildren, either by distance or by inclination. For these grandparents, there is no lure to be found in having children "the second time around." For them, doing it once is all they ever wanted. Some may fear becoming permanent babysitters, or may think that it has been so long since they were with a baby that they wouldn't know what to do. They may feel liberated finally and be living the lives they have always wanted. They may be experiencing a renaissance in their own lives, a remarriage or a divorce that has opened new doors for them. Or they may simply be the type of parents who were never terribly demanding and don't have the wherewithal or inclination to claim time as the grandparents. Though this low-voltage type of parent might have been ideal for a childless couple, the birth of their children may find them wishing for more energy and interest from their parents. This sudden change in their expectations and desires can cause much confusion and stress. It is incumbent upon the couple to make their desires for grandparental contact known, and then be realistic about how and if their parents can meet that request. Some parents need an invitation.

Couples who have boundary-leaping parents may suffer

from a real conflict. They may find themselves torn between their desire to foster and nurture the grandparent/grandchild connection and their need to set limits as parents take their border crossings to often intolerable heights. Though a couple may have previously been able to modify and direct how, when, and where they spent time with their parents, when children enter the picture all bets are off and new laws and rules of the realm must be established. They must be careful not to make laws that legislate their parents out of existence, or they will miss the potential fun of watching their children benefit from a relationship with their folks. They must also make enough rules to ensure that *their* family is always paramount and that it has enough time to build its own sense of identity.

With the status of parents comes a newfound power and responsibility. For the first time, the couple is making all the decisions for another human being. They can control what their child eats, wears, is exposed to, is taught. Of course, parents have the right to make those decisions, and it is here that they often come into conflict with their child's grandparents. Conflict occurs because grandparents and adult children do not always have the same ideas about child-rearing. Just as their parents revert at this time to old, comfortable behaviors, so might one or both members of the couple. Often the catalyst for this regression is the deep yearning for their parents' approval of and respect for their newfound status as parents. It occurs because adult children are seeking the green light, the all-important okay, from their parents about their own approach to parenting. This can be a breeding ground for conflict and disappointment on both sides. It is important for couples to integrate the Power of Parenthood with the "Royal We" of their marriage. Once united, these two elements provide the building blocks for healthy, warm, and realistic encounters with parents of the "grand" kind.

The Power of Parenthood

Like the power of the "Royal We," the Power of Parenthood finds its strength not in overpowering others but in identifying the important issues that affect you as a family and believing in and asserting the right to decide your family's direction. The power comes from a clear consensus between you and your spouse about what is worth fighting over and what can be allowed. It comes from having together determined the level of contact and involvement you both wish from your child's grandparents. It comes from recognizing that in order to reap the benefits of such a relationship, you must bear up under some of the qualities or attitudes of your parents that might be contrary to yours. Flexibility, not rigidity, is the hallmark of power. Flexibility comes from the confidence that your decisions are right for you and your family. However, it also acknowledges that others may not agree with you. Therefore you do not expend energy trying to get your parents to agree with you, but rather you accept that they see things differently. Once that is accomplished, then it is possible to bypass arguments and simply agree to disagree. When you have done that, your parents must play by your rules. Your maturity and your confidence will enable you to allow those rules to be broken on occasion, but not so often that you feel your basic principles are being compromised.

The Early Years

Lisa, the 28-year-old mother of a three-year-old, reports her family's dilemma this way:

"My father-in-law is a lovely man, full of energy and endlessly on the move. That's probably how he got so far in business, made so much money, and was able to retire at the age of 60. He has lots of time on his hands and lots of energy, which he lovingly offers to my daughter, Amanda, without reservation. By that I mean he plays with her, brings her educational toys, takes her to the zoo, sits and draws with her, and is showing her how to write letters. He tells us that this is his opportunity to 'do it right.' My husband, Keith, can attest to that. He pointedly tells me how his father was too busy to spend any time with him as a child. He was a shadow who passed through the house on Sunday afternoons, and that was about it. The problem we have is that I see the relationship between Amanda and my father-in-law as wonderful and exciting. My husband is always critical of him. He thinks he doesn't take proper care of her when he takes Amanda out, lets her eat too much sweet stuff and miss her nap. Personally, I figure a missed nap is worth an afternoon with Grandpa. Now my husband and I are fighting about it, and I feel tense every time my father-in-law comes by to see us. I'm afraid Keith will say something so out of line that it will alienate his dad, and Amanda will ultimately lose out."

Keith and Lisa are faced with the dilemma of many a young couple who are in both the Early Years of their marriage and the early years of child-rearing. Not only are they trying to establish themselves as parents and providers, but they are wrestling with "doing it better" than their own parents. This is a natural inclination, and our ever-expanding knowledge of child development gives today's parents an opportunity to "do it differently." Keith, in particular, was having difficulty defining his role as father, especially since his father not only was taking on an important role in Amanda's life, but was doing some of the things that Keith considered to be his job. He was too busy being a provider to do them himself. In this case, Keith was virtually dripping with resentment toward his father and the neglect he had felt as a child. To add insult to injury, here was his daughter, the light of his life, getting from his dad all the love and attention that he had longed for as a boy. Though he would never want to deprive Amanda of that love, he could only find fault with his father's behavior and even imagined that Amanda was not completely safe with him. In addition, Keith felt that Lisa was coming down on the side of his father, encouraging that relationship and not supporting him.

Lisa was only seeing things from her own perspective. She had had a loving relationship with her grandparents, which she felt had been invaluable to her own development. She simply didn't want to deprive Amanda of what she had known as one of her most precious relationships while growing up. They argued about everything, even how many caramel candies ("I thought we agreed not to allow her to have those kinds of sweets at such a young age!" yelled Keith) his dad had allowed Amanda to consume at the park. That of course was not the issue, although Lisa and Keith agreed that they did feel strongly about it and should talk to his father about never giving Amanda candy like that again. Lisa was designated as Speaker of the House, because at that point Keith was still too resentful of his father to express their wishes without rancor. Lisa was confident that her father-in-law would immediately heed their request. Once they got past that, Lisa was able to ask Keith about the excessive response he was having to the rest of his father's relationship with Amanda.

The Marriage Mirror revealed to Keith the image of himself as a sad little boy, always wishing for his dad's attention and approval. It also revealed a family in which achievement and success were the means to getting acknowledged. True to the family mandate, Keith had been an Ivy Leaguer and a Phi Beta Kappa, and was the head of his own fledgling, but rather successful, financial planning company. This, of course, left him little time at home with Lisa and Amanda, and once he had consulted the Marriage Mirror, he realized that he was creating for himself the same detachment from his child that his father had with him. Here he was, playing by the family rules, and he was going to miss out on Amanda while his father got to be the perfect grandpa.

Redefining *their* family rules was in order for Keith and Lisa. Keith needed to decide how to integrate Amanda and her needs into his life in a way that fit with his own professional and personal needs. His father spending time with Amanda wasn't the issue; it was more about the fact that *he* didn't have enough time with her. Was he going to take back his time with his daughter? Was he willing to spend a little less time at the office in order to enjoy her? Was he willing to go against the family mandate about success and how to achieve it, in order to have time with his own family? Finally, instead of arguing, Lisa and Keith began a dialogue about the type of parents they wanted to be and the kinds of messages they wanted to send to their children about success, work, and family.

Keith decided that he wanted to be the one to take Amanda to the zoo and to make those kinds of memories with her. It meant changing office hours, lightening his caseload, and deflecting questions from his dad about how the business was going to advance if he didn't put in the hours. Now that Lisa understood Keith's needs and wishes, she was able to support him in his responses to his father. They both explained that Keith's decision to take off Saturdays for family days was not going to kill the company. They also decided that certain activities such as Amanda's first carousel ride or pumpkin patch adventure should be left to Lisa and Keith. They wanted to make their unit strong and primary. However, all of this was not easy. Keith's father put a lot of pressure on Keith by continually expressing his concerns about Keith's business. He was hard pressed to understand any formula for success other than the one he had lived by and had taught his children to live by. Keith pointed out to his dad that he didn't want to wait until he was a grandfather himself to "get it right." He wanted to exercise his prerogative as Amanda's father to have that kind of a relationship with her right now. In the end, Keith had to admit that he would never be able to get his dad to agree to his approach, but that it was right for him and Lisa.

Keith's dad still played an important role in Amanda's life. Once Keith had gotten more of what he wanted in his relationship with Amanda, and once he was able to create his own family standard for success, he was able to be flexible about his father's involvement. Ultimately, he was able to allow his dad to join them on a Saturday outing without resentment.

Ostensibly, Keith and Lisa's problem seems to be coping with a high-voltage, contact-hungry grandparent. And, indeed, Keith's dad would probably fit that parental description. However, when the situation is examined closely, the real issues are twofold and simple:

1. Lisa and Keith were letting his father get away with treating Amanda in a fashion that was not in concert with what they felt was right. The more a couple silently endures such a situation, the more small resentments can build into anger. Once the couple comes to a consensus about their family rules and conveys them, it is incumbent upon the grandparents to respect those wishes.

2. Keith's past was getting in the way of his seeing things clearly. It wasn't so much his father's involvement that was getting to him (although the longing to have had a close relationship with his own father never really ceased), but that he was allowing the past to dictate how he was interacting with Amanda and with his dad. Once he looked into the Marriage Mirror and saw how life in his family of origin was prescribing his present existence, he was able to put his energy into action rather than regret.

Rebecca, a 34-year-old social worker who is the mother of a four-year-old, reported how her mother's constant intrusiveness was causing a problem for her and her husband, Eli:

"My husband and I are both very busy people, and over the years my mother has helped us out on many occasions with our son, Max. She and my dad baby-sit for us, and generally are involved in every aspect of Max's life. My mother in particular has this thing with us. She comments on the length of our work hours, implying that she knows Max better than we do. She insinuates herself into every decision we make, whether it's about playgroups or preschools, his friends, or the food he eats. She is most often down on me. It seems that whatever Max and I do together, she claims she has done it too. If he and I draw, she has made even better pictures with him. If he and I make up a song . . . well, you know . . . she has done it and done it better! I'm going out of my mind. But, I feel that I'm stuck, because she does do us a lot of favors, and Max loves her. She is also very loving and sweet with him. They have a wonderful relationship. He doesn't notice what a difficult and annoying woman she can be! I just feel that she always bests me . . . wants to appear to be Max's mother. My husband makes me upset because he feels no compunction about just zapping my mother and telling her to back up. The minute he does that, I find myself defending her and caught between both of them. I just feel like running away."

Eli and Rebecca are caught in a cycle of pseudodisagreement—they near consensus and then veer off into defensiveness. As we've stated before, facing the good and bad traits in your parents is one of the hardest things a person can do. Hearing your parents' faults described eloquently by your spouse can spark a defense that would rival the intensity of the great Clarence Darrow. Difficult as it may be for Rebecca, she needs to take a look at her mother's behavior so that she and Eli can find the negatives and positives about her and develop a common language and understanding. Then they won't find Rebecca suddenly defending her mother from what appear to be Eli's attacks.

In actuality, they both could agree that Rebecca's mother was overbearing and a bit of a loose cannon when it came to them. They could agree that every time she implied that she knew better or was better at doing something with their son, Max, they both felt put down and furious. They could agree that her involvement with Max was overall positive. They could agree that something had to be done so they could better manage her personality and style. They could agree that they wanted to maintain the relationship with Rebecca's mother while minimizing the stress it was putting on their marriage. So what is all this pseudodisagreement about?

Eli is an independent soul. He was used to an open and challenging relationship with his own parents. He had always spoken his mind as a kid, and been respected for it. He never felt at risk when doing it. He has always spoken his mind to Rebecca, and his style of communicating has been very reassuring to her. She knows where she stands with him.

Rebecca is a much more dependent soul. She has always had a relationship with her parents, especially with her mother, that left her feeling inadequate and unsure of her feelings and opinions. She often felt it was fruitless to raise an issue with them, because it usually got turned around and became her problem or her fault.

Eli's natural inclination to speak his mind to his mother-in-law when she stepped on his or Rebecca's emotional toes made Rebecca's hair stand on end. Her natural inclination was to avoid anything that would give her mother reason to put them down or one-up them. Eli's outspokenness would invariably cause her mother to comment on his moodiness or temper in a derogatory way. Rebecca would immediately pick up the tension and put herself in the middle. In the end Eli would be angry with her for trying to lessen the impact of his words on his mother-in-law, and her mother would be finding ways of making Rebecca feel bad for having chosen such an insensitive husband. Sometimes her mother would really throw her hat in the ring and tell Rebecca how hurt and unappreciated she felt, and that maybe she should stop seeing Max altogether. By then alarms would be going off in Rebecca's head, and she would pick a fight with Eli—if she wasn't already in one.

This couple must take some positive action to get themselves out of the cycle of pseudodisagreement, and out of engaging Rebecca's mother in an unproductive way. The first important issue is that, knowingly or unknowingly, they managed to share *all* of their thoughts and every decision they made about Max with Rebecca's mother. *She simply has too much information.* If they plan to have him tested for lyme disease, because he is out in the country a lot over the summer, they tell her—even though the test won't be done for four weeks. Naturally her mother has loads to say about the test, the timing, and the fact that they let him run free in the grass over the summer! If they are looking into a particular play group for him, they let her know what they are thinking—even though their thoughts on the matter are unformed and un*informed* at that point. Naturally, she has opinions about that play group, and runs around to find another, better program for Max. Why is this couple giving Rebecca's mother information about issues that are unclear or undecided between them? Why aren't they waiting to share things with her when they are clearer and possibly already decided?

Eli would say he does this simply because he is used to speaking his ongoing thoughts without somebody jumping to conclusions, offering unwanted opinions, and judging his ideas. Rebecca would say that she is used to sharing her thought process with her parents because she was always raised to doubt her own ideas and to rely on them to set her straight. She would also say that since her mother is with Max so much, she naturally might want to know what they are planning for him.

This couple must learn to withhold information from Rebecca's mother and thereby appoint themselves the prevailing decision-making unit. They need to remind themselves that they are the adults, that they are the parents, and that they must take the responsibility for their choices. This tactic helps Rebecca come to her *own* conclusions before she brings them to her mother. It enables her to break the cycle of self-doubt and dependence on her mother's opinions. For Eli, this strategy allows him to interact more appropriately with his mother-in-law. If he anticipates her behavior, withholds information until he and Rebecca have formed ideas and implemented their plans, he will have fewer opportunities to "zap" her and more opportunities to behave maturely. Eli and Rebecca will feel united and strengthened and less likely to be overturned by Rebecca's mother's style.

In the process, they begin to exercise the Power of Parenthood. Sure, Rebecca's mother is involved with Max, but they are his parents, and they have every right to make decisions about where he will go to school without having to engage her in the discussion. At first, this change will not be easy to implement. Their natural inclination to talk out their decisions in front of Rebecca's mom will have to stop, and that will take some discipline on both their parts. Initially, little phrases will pass their lips that will amount to confessions about what they are planning. The pull toward behaving in old, familiar ways is often overpowering. But with practice and help, there will be fewer such slips and they will begin to feel the appropriateness of forming their own decisions. Once they get really good at becoming a decision-making team, they will be able to be flexible enough to occasionally ask for Rebecca's mother's opinion. After all, she may well have a few good ideas up her sleeve!

A third common scenario that often plagues the parents of young children throughout the years of their marriage is what is known as "dueling grandparents." Talbot, a 31-year-old book jacket designer, relates the problem this way:

"My parents live in Minnesota, so they can only come and visit us three or four times a year. My wife Joy's parents live about 20 minutes away, and we see them what seems like all the time. I feel bad for my folks because they really are dying to be with my kids, but the trip is difficult for them, our house isn't that big, and they can only stay for four or five days at a time because of my dad's work schedule. When they come they bring lots and lots of gifts for the kids, they take them out and will do anything with them and buy them anything. Joy gets angry and says my folks are spoiling them. I figure, heck, they only see them a few times a year, and they might as well have fun. Joy's parents get them things throughout the year . . . maybe not so expensive, but they see them so much more. You are comparing apples and oranges, I tell her. She says her parents feel that they have to compete with the gifts my folks give, but they can't afford it financially. She tells me how unfair it is that just because my parents have more money than hers, they get away with it. We fight every time my parents leave after a visit. I agree the gifts are a bit excessive, but I'll be damned if I'm going to stop them from bringing things. They come a long way at their own expense. My kids really love them, and that's what I want."

Joy and Talbot spent a lot of time arguing over the message his folks were giving the kids by bringing them such expensive gifts. Joy didn't want her in-laws to "buy" the kids' love and affection. She also reminded Talbot that they had agreed that it wasn't good for the kids to receive such costly things without having to work for them. However, Talbot countered with his own concerns that his parents had such little time with the kids that each visit was an accumulation of things they had picked up along the way and they just deposited it all on the kids at the time of the visit. "Your parents bring them lots of things throughout the year and you never say anything about it!" They argued circles around each other, and it was only when Talbot's parents came to visit the next time with an armload of gifts that Joy insisted that she and Talbot at least feel them out about the issues.

Joy brought up the subject one night when the kids were in bed and the four grownups found themselves playing one of the Nintendo games Talbot's parents had brought. She started to talk about how expensive it must be for them to bring all those gifts. With the discussion launched, it became clear that Talbot's parents also felt they were competing with Joy's parents, not for quantity of gifts, but quantity of time spent with the kids. They felt they could never catch up in the hearts of their grandchildren, and so the gifts were a way for them to be remembered even when they weren't there. That night Talbot and Joy talked alone and realized that Talbot had the same competitive feelings on his parents' behalf. He was willing to bend the rule about expensive gifts to make sure they maintained a place in the heart of the children. He felt jealous of the amount of time Joy's parents spent with the kids. He wanted his own parents to be as important and as loved. Joy could understand his longing, but she felt strongly that costly gifts were not the answer. A brainstorming session netted some creative and inexpensive ideas. How about an ongoing letter on cassette tape that would be sent back and forth so that every week the children heard their grandparents' voices? What about a videotape that went back and forth with Grandma reading a book to them on tape or showing them a craft project or a baking project? They could tape themselves at dinner talking about their day and talking to the children. Joy said that she would be willing to make the commitment to help the children keep up their end of this bargain. Talbot was excited by the ideas, and agreed with Joy that this was a better way to keep his parents present in the minds of their children. Next they needed to employ a Speaker of the House, because they didn't want to offend his parents or make them feel unappreciated for all they had done in the past. Joy volunteered, but in the end it was decided that Talbot would speak because he would be seen as the person more likely to have his parents' interests at heart.

As it turned out, Talbot's parents jumped at the ideas. They began talking over one another about what types of things they could videotape for the kids. They were a little hard pressed, however, to see why they had to limit the gifts—after all, they could afford them. It was here that the "Royal We" and the Power of Parenthood came into play to steady Talbot in his resolve. He pointed out to them that as a family, he and Joy felt strongly on this issue. They had made a decision for themselves and for both sets of grandparents, and he hoped they could abide by his family's needs and wishes. He reiterated that if they really wanted to become more involved in the life of the children, then they could more effectively accomplish this through taped letters and conversations than through presents.

Over subsequent visits it became apparent that Joy and Talbot needed to explain to his parents exactly what *too* expensive meant, but eventually they caught on. The videotapes were a great hit. Grandpa is on the third book of the Narnia series by C. S. Lewis. They've all decided that it would be great if he would read all seven books to them on tape. They kids watch part of it every night, and when they get close to the end of a book they call and let him know and he sends on the next installment! They are having a wonderful time.

Grandparents competing for the love and attention of their grandchildren can cause much stress for a couple. Grandparent competition is often a reflection of the couple's own competitive feelings, and this complicates the picture yet more. With Joy and Talbot, it was important that they understand their own feelings about their parents' involvement. It was also necessary that they not undermine their own family rules or the Power of Parenthood to meet the competitive needs of one or both sets of grandparents.

The Middle Years

In today's culture, more and more couples are divorcing and forming what is called a reconstituted or blended family. A divorce or widowhood and remarriage may bring with it new stepchildren and, for your parents, new stepgrandchildren. The complex feelings and logistical arrangements that arise from these blended families are mind-boggling. Negotiating them all with calm, ease, and finesse is nearly impossible. But unity between you and your spouse can give you a good base from which to work. It will also afford you a place of comfort when situations and feelings threaten to overwhelm.

Brenda, a 46-year-old mother of two and stepmother of one, describes her dilemma with her parents this way:

"I remarried two years ago to a man with a young son, Caleb. I have a 10-year-old and a 12-year-old. My parents have always been involved with my kids and are good grandparents. When I divorced, they really helped me out. My husband's parents aren't living, and he sees my parents as his son's opportunity to have grandparents. The problem is that my parents don't seem to pay any real attention to Caleb. I guess they figure that he's not really theirs. Mike's feelings are hurt, and he even said that if my parents didn't accept Caleb then they shouldn't be allowed to see my two children. His frustration just pours out of him! I feel in the middle, because quite frankly I understand my parents feeling distant from Caleb, but you know, I want Mike to be happy. I am always defending my parents' position when we fight, I guess because I don't really know what to do about it."

Brenda and Mike have been allowing Brenda's folks to treat Mike and Caleb as second-class citizens, as if they were outsiders in the family. The grandparents act as if only Brenda and her two kids form the nuclear unit. It often takes a long time before the couple's two families stop orbiting one another and actually become one integrated family. If it's difficult for the couple who are doing this by choice, you can imagine the dilemma this poses when grandparents try to adapt to the new family unit.

The most important aspect of this situation was that Mike and Brenda had allowed Brenda's folks to dictate who actually constituted the family. They also had not clarified with each other their own expectations regarding grandparental involvement with their new blended bunch. At the same time, Brenda was not clear in her allegiance. She was feeling torn because at the time of her divorce, she had realigned herself with her parents and they had helped her a great deal. Now that she was married again, she was hard pressed to realign herself with Mike. She felt like she would be betraying the two people who had helped her through a rough time. Mike, on the other hand, was feeling more and more angry that Brenda wasn't with him on this, and *he* felt betrayed.

At this late stage of her life, Brenda was about to go through what young marrieds usually must attend to—she had to renegotiate her attachments and align herself with Mike. She had done it in her first marriage, though not terribly successfully, and now here she was doing it again at 45 years of age! She was experiencing all the feelings that a 20-year-old bride might have about loosening the ties of allegiance to her parents. Of course Brenda had to pledge herself to Mike and Caleb, or the marriage would be in dire straits. And simultaneously, she had to loosen her ties to her parents without losing them. A plenary meeting revealed these issues, and also made it clear that she and Mike had to be crystal clear about what it was they expected, wanted, or hoped for from her parents. Most important, they had to be realistic, because it is difficult if not impossible to force people to love one another. It takes lots of time to build a relationship of trust and love. Mike, in particular, had to accept that right up front. He had to think in terms of small steps forward that he would like to see in the relationship between Brenda's folks, himself, and Caleb.

Besides the natural and important desires this couple had about wanting to become and be treated as a whole family, their reflections in the Marriage Mirror showed them why their situation was so difficult and where their expectations were coming from. Mike's look in the Mirror revealed the image of his own widowed father marrying a woman with four children. Mike and his brother were always called "the boys." Their stepmother never made any real attempt to know them, though she certainly didn't neglect their physical care. Mike always felt that he had lost his father to this woman, because his father never insisted that she pay any real attention to who his sons were as people, or what their emotional needs might be. It was a kind of emotional abandonment. Mike saw at that moment that his inability to completely align himself with Brenda came out of his fear that Caleb would feel left behind or abandoned. He wanted Brenda and her parents to take them as a package deal.

Brenda's look in the Marriage Mirror revealed a family with two divorces in it, hers and that of her sister Irene. Irene had never remarried, and her parents played a large role in her family with her three kids as well. Brenda realized that at the time of her own divorce there was an unspoken understanding that the family would stick together and take care of each other. It had become commonplace for them to think of themselves as a large unit. They joked that they should call themselves the Ten McCloughlins and form a singing group. She realized that her resistance to aligning herself with Mike and Caleb came from the intense gravitational pull of the Ten McCloughlins. She wasn't a McCloughlin any longer, but unless she realigned herself, that change would be in name only.

It was determined at their plenary meeting that Brenda would be the Speaker of the House. They felt that only a McCloughlin would be heard in that tight circle. Also, Brenda felt that she could better explain how much this meant to her and Mike without expressing disapproval about how they had been behaving up till now. Brenda had to watch out for her own resistance to giving up her position in the McCloughlin family circle. One thing she could count on was the knowledge that her parents had always wanted her to be happy and that their love for her should win out in the end. Mike and Brenda set a small goal for the meeting. They hoped that Brenda would come away from it with her parents understanding more about the importance of her relationship with Mike and Caleb, and possibly a commitment to spending a bit more time with Caleb.

Brenda broached the subject of Mike and Caleb. She began by acknowledging how difficult it was at first for her to include Mike and Caleb into the McCloughlins' tight family group. This was a very important first step. *Before requesting changed behavior from parents, it is imperative that the couple take responsibility for their own behavior and attitudes that might be contributing to the problem. By doing this, they take the onus off the parents in a way that frees them to listen. It sends the message that everyone will have to work to remedy the unwanted situation.*

A discussion ensued that was difficult and at times painful

to hear. She listened as her parents told her that they were tired, and Caleb was so young it was like starting over with a grandchild again. They also revealed that they had been attached to her first husband, that the breakup had been difficult for them, and they were hard pressed to give their hearts to another. Brenda had to hold onto her chair as she heard all of this, so that she wouldn't say anything that might put them on the defensive. She spoke of her understanding of their feelings, how difficult it is to mandate a relationship, and how she too had had to learn to love Caleb. She told them how important their being a part of her family was both to her and the children, and that now her family consisted of Mike and Caleb. With Mike's permission, she told them about his childhood and how he had felt abandoned by his father for not insisting that his second wife take the time to get to know his children. She ended by asking them to just think a bit about what she had said. She decided not to extract a commitment from them about their relationship with Caleb at that time, because she sensed that they had a lot of information to digest. By handling the situation in this manner, Brenda was beginning the dialogue. She was setting in motion the "legwork" that would be necessary to enact true change in everyone's behavior. It is important for couples to have a realistic expectation of how change can and will occur with their parents. Expecting things to change less and more slowly than you might wish is probably an excellent idea. If a couple enters these dialogues with their parents knowing that actual change will probably fall short of their ideal, it leaves them free of the weight of disappointment.

One woman, Camille, reported that the discord in her marriage in the Middle Years came from her second husband being regarded as the "honored guest" by her parents:

"My husband, Joe, is a good man, a wonderful stepfather, and is adored by my parents. They hated my first husband, and Joe is a refreshing change for them. Since we have been married, he can do no wrong. If he fixes my mother's toaster, he becomes God's gift to creation. Truthfully, it has made me a little angry. I get the feeling that my parents like and respect Joe more than they do me. I've been able to keep all those feelings tucked away, because we didn't live close to them, didn't see them that often, and frankly, I think Joe is a pretty terrific guy myself. Recently, circumstances have changed. I've gone back to work, and my parents moved to our town. My mother has generously agreed to come by every day after school to watch the kids till Joe or I get home. The kids love having her there, and she feels very useful. The problem I have is that she seems to pick up on every difference Joe and I have about rearing the kids. For example, Joe thinks it's okay for the kids to ride bikes when they get home and do their homework *after* dinner. In general I also think it's okay too but my daughter has some difficulty and needs that extra time to focus on what she is doing. My mother knows how I feel about this but will not enforce my rule. Instead she will invoke Joe's name when I ask her why Carol is still outside when I get home at six o'clock. If Joe and I differ slightly on something we say to the kids, my mom will side with Joe. Frankly, I'm tired of it. Joe doesn't see it. He thinks my mom is wonderful. Why wouldn't he? It seems to be a mutual admiration society!"

The real problem here is not with Camille's parents. Many parents see their sons-in-law or daughters-in-law as honored guests. This can be especially striking in a second marriage, where the new spouse is beloved, seen as a savior, and compares favorably to the previous spouse. Because these spouses maintain a position of guest, they are accorded all the allowances and unconditional approval that a guest or friend might receive. Their glow is never tarnished by disagreement or even reality. They are kept on a pedestal, and can't be knocked off. Inevitably, their partners become jealous of this enviable position, and they are often the ones who try to knock them off the pedestal. They will sometimes do this by bad-mouthing them to their parents in an attempt to tarnish their good name. More often than not, they will end up fighting with their spouse out of frustration with the situation.

Indeed, the work that this couple needed to do was strictly between themselves. They had no reason to confront Camille's mother about anything. One look in the Marriage Mirror found Camille faced with her own grandmother's adoration of her son-in-law, her father. She had accepted this as a child and, in fact, felt her father completely deserving of such a position. It was odd to acknowledge that her mother had simply imitated her grandmother's approach to the son-in-law. Camille wondered if her mother had ever experienced some of the pangs of jealousy that she herself felt now.

Joe's look in the Mirror reflected a family in which his father was a kind of nonentity. He was a bland man who could be found sitting in the reclining chair, watching TV. His parents' marriage was not a particularly happy one. It was more of an endurance test. Joe had always been a help to his mother and knew how to make her happy with his jokes and good-natured style. Naturally, this style carried over in his interactions with Camille's parents, especially her mother.

Camille had to admit that part of what was attractive about Joe was that he was a lot like her father. Joe had to admit that winning mother's approval was where he put all his energy as a kid, and he was still doing it. But what of his wife's approval? Actually, Joe assumed he *had* Camille's approval. He had no reason to think otherwise, because Camille had never told him how she felt about his role as the honored guest. Up until now, Joe had been unable to see that by *siding* with his mother-in-law, or unconsciously enjoying it when she sided with him over Camille, he was getting his own gratification at the expense of his wife's feelings. Only when Camille found the courage to face her own feelings about the situation and discuss them with Joe were they able to come to an understanding. They came to a consensus about how the past was affecting their present, and they were able to offer each other more support—especially in front of Camille's parents. She no longer felt the need to knock Joe off his pedestal.

They worked scrupulously at the task before them. They spoke with one voice, gave one set of instructions to Camille's mother about child care, and joined forces with each other. What Joe may have lost in "guest" status, he more than gained back by winning his wife's happiness.

The Later Years

The Later Years of your marriage will find you with aging parents who have mortality issues gnawing at them on a daily basis. Their friends are dying, their health may be failing, and their physical and emotional world is becoming more and more circumscribed. Sometimes, their money constitutes their last bastion of control. For grandparents who are no longer blessed with an everyday role or even a necessary role with their grandchildren, money can be a way for them to keep connected.

Victoria and Colin found themselves faced with this as their children, already in their early twenties, were being "grandparented" in ways with which they did not agree.

"I've been very angry with my wife's parents," reported Colin, a city desk editor for a medium sized newspaper, five years away from his own retirement. "I've worked damned hard all my life to provide for them and I expect them to have the same drive and ideas about work. My in-laws are pretty wealthy, and it took Vicky and me years to rein in their expensive gift-giving and promises to the kids. We thought we had it licked until the other day. My father-in-law just informed my three kids that he has set up a trust for each of them, and that at the age of 25 they will each be receiving a huge lump sum inheritance. They are talking about a good deal of money. It's their money to do with what they want, but it just seems irresponsible to drop a lump sum on young people before they've had a chance to make their way. I'm afraid it will make my kids lazy and short-circuit their careers. Easy money is how I see it, and I don't think it's good for them. Vicky agrees, but she doesn't feel we have any rights . . . she defends them. I think if they really loved the kids they would handle the money issue differently."

What is a viable plan of action for Vicky and Colin in this situation? After all, the children are adults. Vicky's parents have every right to leave their money as they see fit. By now Vicky and Colin have done their parenting job as best they can. This is not an issue much in their control. On top of that, Vicky and Colin disagree about how they perceive the situation, and until they find common ground, nothing should be done. After wrangling for a while, they sat down to discuss the issue. Colin expressed his point of view:

1. The grandparents spoke directly to the grandchildren without first mentioning their intentions to Vicky and Colin.
2. The structure of the bequest meant that the children, at a young age, would have to manage and integrate a large sum of money into their work ethic.
3. He felt that all their years of teaching their children about the importance of career and work were going to be undermined.

4. He felt one-upped by his father-in-law because he could not leave that kind of money for his kids or potential grandkids.
5. Finally, he was upset that Vicky seemed to be so passive about it all and didn't appear to be on his side.

Vicky felt differently:

1. Wealth had neither warped nor destroyed her own sense of the importance of work when she was growing up.
2. She felt powerless and that she had no right to influence her parents' decisions about this issue.
3. She and Colin had always known there would be some inheritance, so why was he acting so surprised and upset about it now?

The Marriage Mirror was a useful place for them to start, since they could not find common ground during their talk. Colin came from a working-class background in which his father slaved away to get him and his sister educated and on their way to a "better life." He had watched his father work two jobs when they were in college, without any complaints. His mother was a homemaker until they were teenagers, and then she went to work as an aide in a hospital. Hard work was admired; sloth was looked down on. He felt strongly that though his children had it easier, they could still benefit from learning the value of hard work and the joys of having a career.

Vicky's glance in the Mirror revealed a life in which she had all the advantages of wealth. Her parents had not come from wealthy backgrounds, and so underlying their generosity was a message that if you worked hard you could make it. Vicky and her siblings had watched their father work like a dog to build his financial nest egg. Each of them had worked at his company every summer as they got old enough. Each of them was asked to earn at least part of the money for items their parents felt were above and beyond what they considered ordinary expenses.

Colin had always known in the back of his mind that his in-laws would be giving the kids money one day, and maybe that's why he was so passionate about making sure the kids did chores at home from a young age, worked during summers off from school, took out partial loans for college, and generally were made to act responsibly toward money and the family. Vicky had never really worried about the inheritance, because she had come from a household with a clear sense about a work ethic. If she hadn't, she never could have married a man like Colin, whose fortune would never equal that of her father's. She had always admired Colin's willingness to work hard and maintain good, solid values.

After talking, Vicky and Colin remembered that though their childhoods had been spent in different financial strata, their values had always been very much in line. Once that bit of consensus was reached, they could face more of the real issue at hand. Could they trust that the lessons they had taught their children would be retained by them in the face of a large inheritance? Could they speak to Vicky's parents about how they would administer the money? They decided that they had very little real power, now that their children were adults, to monitor the children's interaction with their grandparents. They did, however, agree that they needed to have a friendly discussion with her parents to express their concerns and offer a solution to what they felt was too much, too soon. Vicky was designated Speaker of the House, but for this discussion she needed much support from Colin. A nongrudging appreciation for their generosity and their well-meaning gestures was the tone of the meeting. A suggestion for spreading out the payments to the children was made. This was all that Vicky and Colin could do with her parents. Then they had to go one step further and talk openly with their children about their concerns. In this situation, as in many situations concerning grandparents, a couple may have little actual right or power to effect a change. But they can change the way they relate to each other in the context of such a difficult situation. They can reach a consensus. They can support each other, and they can do what it takes to keep sending appropriate messages to their children.

The Power of Parenthood holds one last trump card: Parents are the ultimate influencers of children. Most of the time children go through adulthood with their parents' values, morals, and ethics securely in their heads and hearts. Grandparents sometimes offer a break from those views, but they almost never hold the sway or influence that parents do. Parents must love and guide their children, while grandparents only need to love them. The first is a much harder job that in the end is usually appreciated by most children. The unfettered love of grandparents holds a special but different place in the heart of a child. In the end, children develop and are formed by the parents' love and values, seasoned gently by the love and attention of grandparents.

CHAPTER ELEVEN

Aging Parents — Family Helping Family

"I believe that every right implies a responsibility;
every opportunity, an obligation; every possession,
a duty."
John D. Rockefeller, Jr.[19]

Never before have so many people lived to such advanced ages. More and more couples are being asked to meet the challenge of their parents' increasing age and needs. This obligation is an important part of family life that cannot be ignored. Commitments to meeting it have often been cast as a dark, unrelenting duty, and indeed, couples are often asked to take on tasks that are burdensome and difficult. However, if you have learned to clear away the cobwebs of the past and come to consensus with your spouse, and you are clear about your allegiance to your marriage, you are ready to meet the necessary and inevitable obligations of family life. With the advantage of having a relationship with one's parents comes the sometimes inconvenient and time-consuming task of family supporting family.

At first, most couples feel blindsided by the increased demands and pressures of dealing with aging parents. (This stage in a couple's marriage may be the most difficult when it comes to balancing the sacrifices of family obligation without sacrificing their marriage.) Dramatic events such as widowhood, illness, and death often require an instantaneous response. If a father is recently widowed and is ill equipped to manage his home, then immediate steps must be taken to remedy the situation. If your parent is suddenly rendered infirm, and must come and live with you, there can be unspeakable strain that might only be addressed after the practical deed is done and the parent is ensconced in the spare room upstairs. Rarely do people speak of the advantages of these relationships in the same breath with which they speak of the strain, tension, and burden of them. But when meeting any type of family obligation a couple must do three things: 1. protect the integrity of their marriage; 2. discover the positive aspects that meeting this obligation brings to the family as a whole; and 3. learn the art of patience and compassion, for therein lies the key to finding the balance and self-respect to successfully progress through this phase of the marital journey. One other major stress inevitably arises during this stage of life: the death of a parent. The influence of a deceased parent is as powerful as, if not more powerful than, that of a living, breathing person. Much attention should be paid by the couple to the real role this ongoing relationship plays in their marriage.

Dealing with an aging parent presents a unique set of problems in every stage of married life. In the Early Years, the sudden illness or death of an aging parent can strain the already fragile hold a couple has on their allegiance to each other and their building a sense of the "Royal We." In the Middle Years, couples who are raising families and careers may be asked to protect and care for a parent. Here too the sheer amount of work necessary to meet the needs of so many can put incredible pressure on a marriage. In the Later Years, just when a couple is beginning to breathe easy and plan their unfettered future together, dreams of retirement can be snuffed out by the needs of an aged parent. Lost dreams and unfulfilled hopes can send a marriage off course.

The Early Years

Throughout this book, the ultimate importance of establishing true allegiance and the Royal We in a marriage has been made clear. The necessity of renegotiating attachments in the Early Years of a marriage should be seen as tantamount to eating and drinking. Many things can conspire to derail a couple as they attempt to forge this significant connection with each other. One such obstacle is the death of a parent. When a couple starts out, they define their sense of "Royal We" by separating from their parents. When a parent dies as this separation is taking place, problems can arise because it is very common for a child to introject that parent's ideas, morals and behaviors. It is a psychologically efficient way to keep the departed person with you. A byproduct of this introjection is the increasing "presence" of the deceased in your behavior, your thinking, and your attitude. This overlaying of your parent's life onto your own makes it difficult to know how you feel about things, and consequently makes it difficult for you and your spouse to forge your own views together.

John, a 27-year-old teacher and soccer coach, reported the problem this way:

> "My wife's mother died about six months after we got married. We've been married for two years now. Before she died, she and my wife had a sometimes stormy relationship. My wife was pretty independent of her and spoke her own mind. My mother-in-law always put in her two cents. When we went to look for a house to buy, she was *more* than clear that she thought we should buy a town house. It seemed to us that she was saying that we didn't have the knowhow or wherewithal to manage

our own home. She also tried to approach us from the practical side . . . that we both worked and it would be a big-time commitment to have our own house. Rita and I were clear. When my mother-in-law died, we stopped looking for a house . . . just put it on hold. Now that we have begun looking again, I can't believe my ears. Rita has decided that we need to buy a town house. The words that are coming out of her mouth make me wonder if her mother is still alive! They sound exactly the same. We are fighting a lot now about all sorts of things that I thought we had agreed on before. She's changed, and I don't like it."

What John is experiencing is the loss of the consensus that he felt he had established with his wife. He thought he knew where the two of them stood and that they were united. Where does this sudden change come from? First, the previous consensus might have been based more on rebellion than on true unity of thinking. It could be that all along Rita was simply taking the opposite stance from her mother as a way of defining herself. Because this stance happened to coincide with John's, it looked as if they had built a consensus. Second, there is a maturation process that takes place in everyone. Rita's shift in position may have been informed by the evolution in her thinking and the experience of her daily life. She may have reassessed how she felt about the demands of homeownership based on the experience of living the demands of her already full life. Third, the shift may have occurred because for Rita, one of the ways to preserve her mother is to preserve her point of view and attitudes. This subtle and unconscious shift must be understood as a part of the spouse's grieving process. The ability of John and Rita to come to a consensus will be sorely strained until they sort out these three issues.

Couples will sometimes report ease at building a consensus in the Early Years of their relationship. As the years go on they find increasing difficulty in attaining one voice. That early facility is what often draws people to each other. "We agree on everything," the young bride will sing when asked about conflict or point of view in her marriage. Not to be discounted, this early "agreement" does hold water as the basis for future consensus. However, as a couple matures together, they individualize their thinking more and more. Life experiences inform them, and since they have different roles within the family and different jobs outside it, they necessarily have different influences working upon them. Though young couples would like to believe it, two people are rarely of one mind and are rarely of one experience. For Rita and John, they may be coming up on their first experience of individuation in their marriage. And since every time Rita speaks the voice of her mother emerges, they must address the influence her mother's death has wrought in these early years of their marriage.

When they looked back on the death of her mother, they were able to see just how difficult it had been. Sudden and shocking, the death left them both spinning. Rita's relationship with her mother was a complex one, and the death left her with many unresolved issues. This complicated her grieving process, which was characterized by regret and a longing for what could have been, but wasn't to be, between them. For his part, John had only known Rita's mother for about two years before she died, and because of Rita's own strained relationship with her, he never attempted to get terribly close. Her death meant more to him from the point of view of what it meant to Rita. He directed all his energy toward coping with her reaction and her feelings. He didn't experience his own grief.

A grieving spouse exerts a heavy strain on a marriage during this period. Sadness, depression, withdrawal, and great neediness can strain any marriage, but especially one in its earliest years. Rita and John had barely gotten the rhythm of their own marriage going before it was thrown off by

Rita's distress and melancholy. John didn't really know how to comfort her, and he was confused. If Rita's relationship with her mom was so difficult, why was she so sad and miserable? There were times when she wanted his attention and times when her pain left her inaccessible. He was hard pressed to know when to give and exactly how. He saw his carefree days with her disappearing under a fog of grief. He was often short-tempered and unsupportive because of the push and pull of Rita's grief. He wanted his wife back the way she used to be.

Unable to find consensus anywhere in their marriage, they realized that the most important thing for them to do was to come to a consensus about how the grieving was affecting their marriage. With some guidance they were able to recognize the voice of Rita's mother and how it had come to play a part in their difficulty in forming a consensus. It turned out that Rita had always grudgingly heard what her mother had said about their purchasing a house and had given it some unconscious credence. It was hard for her to acknowledge her living mother as having a good point, but now that she was dead, it seemed that Rita was freed to take on her mother's position without having to give her the satisfaction of agreeing with her in person. Macabre, you might think, but it's a common scenario. The death of a parent can free an adult child to take a position previously unthinkable.

Once this problem was opened to discussion, Rita and John were able to find a common ground and a common language to talk and even laugh about her mother's voice and point of view invading their home. It was only a beginning, but it gave the hope that they would be able to find consensus again in their marriage. John, feeling more hopeful, became less tense and more giving. Rita was able to recognize her mother's voice when it piped in and began to separate out what *she* really felt about issues before them.

The Middle Years

"Caught between a rock and a hard place" is how Sybil, a wife, part-time secretary and mother of three children, first described her situation as tears cascaded down her cheeks. She was at a complete loss:

"I'm at the end of my rope. I have three kids, ages twelve, nine, and seven, and I work four mornings a week as a secretary at their school. With the kids alone you can imagine how I spend my days. Laundress, chauffeur, healer, evening faculty at homework time, chief cook and bottle washer, and disciplinarian. My husband works really long hours at his job. I can't blame him; we're lucky he has a good position. But that leaves me with very little support from him, except on the weekends. Now his father has come to live with us, and I am at my wits' end. My mother-in-law died recently, and he wasn't managing well emotionally on his own, so my husband suggested that he move into the extra room downstairs. We had a little kitchen put in to let him have his independence. Once he got here, I realized he needed more attention than I had anticipated. He is upstairs looking for company— he eats most of his meals with us—and now he has taken to interjecting his opinions about my cooking, my discipline of the kids, and he requests being taken all over town to do his "errands." My husband isn't home when these discussions take place. Last week I lost it and yelled at my father-in-law and I felt just awful afterwards. I've been trying to get Dennis to do something about the situation, but he thinks it will just work itself out. I'm furious with him. I'm short with the kids and always feeling torn about what I need to be doing . . . stop and take care of Dennis's dad or take care of the kids and the house."

Sybil is a perfect example of someone living the quintes-
sential "sandwich generation" lifestyle. Although for centuries adult children have been asked to take on the role of
caretakers of ailing or aging parents, it is the current generation that often is sandwiched between the care of these
parents and their own young children. Couples have waited
longer to have children because women have forged careers
that they cherish and nurture, often delaying the starting of
a family until they are in their late twenties or thirties. At
age 40, many of them find themselves working, raising
young children, and staring at the faces of aging parents.
Couples are meeting obligations at both ends of the family
continuum. Too often little regard is paid to the stresses on
their marriage as they race through every day trying to simply survive the demands and needs of their now overflowing
lives.

Once Sybil could corner her husband for a discussion
about the situation, he was able to agree that there was a
problem, though he still felt that things would work themselves out. Frustrated with that response, Sybil pressed for
more time to discuss it. She wasn't satisfied that they had
any real resolution, though they had reached a consensus
that there was a problem. At their next "meeting" two weeks
later, they decided to use the Marriage Mirror as a tool. Sybil
found herself looking at a family of dedicated wives and
mothers who perpetually carried a heavy burden. She saw
her grandmother, an immigrant accustomed to work and
sacrifice. She was self-sufficient, asking little help from anyone, maybe because she knew others were too busy to give
her a hand. Her own mother not only helped her father in
his drapery business, but also took care of her own father
once her mother passed away. Sybil's father was a pleasant
but extremely busy man who came home exhausted from a
day of work. Despite this, their house was full of laughter
and companionship. When her parents had a conflict or an
issue, they often would joke about it, and somehow they

would come to an understanding. Sybil couldn't figure out exactly how. Sybil realized too that she was nearly full grown and out of the house when her grandfather came to live with them. Her own children were still quite young, making her situation very different.

Dennis looked in the mirror and found a similar but less amiable family situation. Both parents worked hard, and were devoted to the family, but there were no avenues for discussion. His father was often noncommunicative and his mother gave up asking him about anything after a while. There was little playful chiding, which is often the tool families use to open discussions and get themselves heard. Silence and the motto "It will work itself out" were the two things he could remember about his family.

Sybil and Dennis were still at a loss. Sybil couldn't emulate her parents' knack for getting heard and getting help from each other, and Dennis felt blighted by his family's lack of communication skills, knowing that he shared their weakness. But hope always rises from consensus, and they could agree on a few things. First, they both came from families in which meeting family obligations and bearing up under the burden was expected. Second, neither family had made direct and clear requests for help. Third, their families of origin were never sandwiched between aging parents and young children in quite the way that they were. They saw their situation as different and therefore subject to the possibility of a new and different response. Joined in adversity, so to speak, they found a kind of unity they had not had before.

They agreed to break the family mold by keeping discussion open about the subject of Dennis's dad and the pressures on Sybil. They agreed that they needed to find solutions to ease the extraordinary burdens Sybil carried. They agreed to hold a weekly plenary meeting until they were able to come up with a solution. Weeks passed, and like most couples, they found things getting in the way of their planned meetings. A crisis needed to develop in order for them to make a change. One afternoon Sybil arrived home from her job, loaded down with groceries and her seven-year-old, whom she had picked up at school because he had a fever. At that moment her father-in-law came upstairs and asked her to drive him to the library so that he could take out some more books. She blew her stack. Didn't he see that she had a sick child, a kitchen full of groceries and three loads of laundry looming in front of her before she could even begin to think about what he wanted? True to his family tradition, Dennis's father wanted to avoid conflict, so he fell silent and returned downstairs. Sybil was furious, not only with herself, but with him for not being more aware of the family around him.

Spurred on by this event, she grabbed Dennis the minute he came in the door and said, "Tonight is the night . . . we work this out or I'll end up in a loony bin." After everyone else had gone to sleep, they had their meeting. It was clear that Dennis's dad displayed the attitude of a guest rather than a member of the family. He had always worked hard, but once he got home, he was used to being taken care of. This would not work if he was to live with them. At the same time, it was clear that there had to be alternative sources of help to ease the burden on Sybil. And finally, Dennis realized that he would have to pick up some of the slack with his dad. They decided that he would look into senior citizen organizations that offered day excursions or transport to the library and other places. They decided to give him specific tasks that would help ease Sybil's burden but would not put too much stress on him. They decided to remember that they needed time together to renew their marriage and keep communication open. They could not decide on a Speaker of the House, so they broached these subjects with him together.

Dennis and Sybil sat down with his dad and explained how glad they were to have him downstairs and available to them and the children. (They broached the subject by first recognizing his importance to them.) Then they described how strained each of them was in meeting all the needs of the children, the home, and their jobs. (They carefully left him out when they spoke of obligations.) They asked if they could have his help since he was there a lot and had a bit of free time. Couched in the language of his being an essential part of the family and the children's lives, they asked if he would be willing to do two things for them: 1. Occasionally, oversee their twelve-year-old when she baby-sat for the younger two children while Sybil and Dennis got a night out together, and 2. Help put away packages and groceries for Sybil when she did her weekly grocery shopping. Much to their surprise, he was delighted. He had been feeling guilty that he was living off them and didn't know how to go about offering to help (except through his "suggestions" about how Sybil was doing things). Then they mentioned that they had contacted a senior citizen organization and found out there was a van that twice weekly took seniors into town to do errands. One of the stops was the library. They suggested to him that there would be times when Sybil would simply be too occupied to take him to town, and he might consider using the senior citizen bus. At first he balked because he didn't see himself as anything like "those old people," but when the idea was presented to him from the point of view of easing some of the stresses in the family, he said he would give it a try.

From these small beginnings, they were able to work toward clearer communication with each other and with Dennis's dad about their living situations. Most important, Sybil and Dennis had developed a language for discussing their family and marital situation. They were no longer fighting over these issues. At last Sybil felt heard and supported by Dennis! This was a step toward meeting their family obligations without sacrificing their marriage.

The Later Years

Charlotte and Ken were both 65 and proud of it. They had spent years poring over an atlas of the United States in anticipation of their retirement gift to themselves, a year-long cross-country tour. They had purchased a used Winnebago a few years back, and had painstakingly refurbished the inside themselves so they could keep their costs down. In another six months they would be on the road. They had bought a cell phone so that their grown children could keep track of them. Charlotte's mother, who was 85, resided in an assisted living facility that she had arranged for years ago. She was secure there, and so they were all set to go—no worries, no guilt, no fear! One day they received a call from the home and found out that Charlotte's mother had had a stroke and would need to be moved out of the assisted living facility because she now required too much care for them to manage her. She would have to be sent to a nursing home. After a time, sadness was replaced by reality. Her mother's expenses at the assisted living facility had been paid by Medicaid, and though the benefits would eventually kick in for the nursing home, they discovered that entry fees needed to be paid if they wanted her to go to a home of good quality. These fees amounted to tens of thousands of dollars. All of their extra money had been earmarked for their cross-country adventure, and they were panicked as they began to see their dream disappearing before their eyes.

Ken reports the stress on their marriage this way:

> "Charlotte has been a complete wreck since her mother had the stroke. She is hysterical about finding the right nursing home and spends every waking hour reading pamphlets from the government on services they offer, and nursing home brochures. The nursing homes are all about the same, so I don't get the problem. Nothing seems to suit her, and time is running short. She has

started yelling at me for the slightest thing . . . and lately she accused me of not saving enough money along the way so we would have extra for a time like this. Now I'm a spendthrift! I'm furious with her sister who lives in Arizona and hasn't lifted a finger to come up or help Charlotte to make any decisions . . . out of sight, out of mind I guess. I've told Charlotte that if her sister and brother-in-law don't pitch in some money to help out, I'm giving nothing . . . let Medicaid figure it out!"

Alarms are going off in Ken and Charlotte's house. Because so many of us are living longer, we are reaching our own retirement and finding that we have an aged parent still living and in need of care. It is an extremely difficult position, but not an uncommon one. For a couple like Ken and Charlotte, who have been so allied in trying to make their retirement dream happen, the tension is extraordinary. Ken sees his dream of wide open spaces and leisurely drives through the gorgeous countryside vanishing before his eyes. It came as a complete shock to Ken that Charlotte didn't think as he did about this issue. After all, they both wanted this trip so badly. Charlotte equates Ken's ultimatum about money with his forsaking her mother and her. Charlotte is torn between allegiance to her mother and her own dreams and allegiance to Ken. It had been a long time since anything had happened to test their pledge of allegiance. In fact, if you compared them to other couples in their social group, they seemed to have the marriage most dedicated to the idea of the "Royal We" and clear allegiance. Imagine living together for 42 years and not having to test the strength of that allegiance till now. They were sorely out of practice!

Ken moped around, feeling betrayed by Charlotte and furious with her sister. Charlotte was in a frenzy, and she hardly noticed what she was doing to Ken and to their marriage. All she could do was press ahead and look for the perfect nursing home. It had been so long since they had been at opposite ends of an issue that Ken hardly knew how to approach Charlotte. He could only express his rage at her sister. Charlotte felt he didn't understand the gravity of her mother's situation and was only focused on money.

The couple blamed each other for this predicament. Charlotte blamed Ken for not saving enough money along the way. Ken blamed Charlotte for getting "so hysterical" and jeopardizing their trip, and he blamed Charlotte's sister for not helping out. Blaming is a tool of resistance, because it rarely gets you close enough to the issue at hand to actually solve a problem. It also distracts a couple from the real task at hand: coming together to solve the problem.

When they sat down to discuss the situation calmly (with some help from a therapist), they attempted to reframe each other's behavior. What was most evident was the grief they were each experiencing. Ken grieved for his mother-in-law, but mostly for the long-awaited trip he wanted so desperately to take with his wife. Charlotte was grieving for the trip, but mostly for her mother and the loss of function her mother was now experiencing. Each had replaced the expression of that grief with angry exchanges and frustrated behavior. Once they understood that they each were experiencing a loss, they were able to have a little more empathy for each other.

It was suggested to them that they not try to handle the situation on their own—to which Ken replied that Charlotte's sister was no help at all. Charlotte, of course, began to defend her sister from Ken's attack (a pseudodisagreement if ever there was one). It was suggested that Charlotte's sister might not be the only person available to help them at this time. What about their children? It had never occurred to them to talk to their children (now grown and in their thirties and forties) to see if they had any ideas or could offer financial assistance for their grandmother's care. It was difficult for them to turn to their children. They had always been able to take care of things and help their children in times of need, not the other way around. However, the only way to solve the problem was to pull together like a family. They gave themselves permission to: 1. have the right to their retirement dream, and 2. rely on family helping family at this difficult time.

The situation turned out more positively than they could have imagined once they allowed themselves to talk to their children. One of their daughters-in-law had a friend whose father worked at an excellent nursing home. He had offered to see if he could get Charlotte's mother admitted there. The entrance fees in Virginia were a lot lower than where they had been looking. They were a little upset that the home was in Virginia, but they would be traveling for the next year anyway, and their son and daughter-in-law lived nearby. They could check in on Grandma every now and again. The entry fees Charlotte and Ken paid to the nursing home meant they had to cut back their trip by a full six weeks, but in the end it was a small price to pay to have what they both wanted—excellent care for Charlotte's mother and their retirement ramble across the country.

There is no magical answer to this last phase of parental influence on a marriage. There is only the final opportunity to limit the stress on your marriage while fulfilling the obligations of family helping family. In order to get the full benefit of the parental relationship for yourself, your spouse and your children, it is necessary to make sacrifices. Those sacrifices enrich, test, and broaden relationships within the family, but, as always, a couple must know the difference between family sacrifice and sacrifice of their marriage. With that in mind, modulating the impact of all of life's many obligations upon your marriage is a reasonably attainable goal.

Some Final Reflections

"The best way out is always through."
Robert Frost[20]

You can begin to know your own marriage when you and your spouse examine the looking glass that reflects each of your family's histories and styles. There you will find all the information you will need about parents' attitudes and behaviors as well as details about your role in your original family. This knowledge will bring you closer to your objective of strengthening your marriage and negotiating the relationship you have with your parents and in-laws. By taking that information and using it to secure marital allegiance and consensus, your marriage can find its voice and its way. By respecting the bonds you have to your parents, you can build a peacefully co-existing, multigenerational family.

Instituting plenary meetings will allow you to reach consensus and set your goals. The use of early warning systems and diplomatic delivery of your decisions will allow you to effect long-lasting change. And through holding your ground in the face of everyone's resistance, you will meet with success. Learning to have a private laugh about some of your parents' more difficult or bothersome behavior will help to get you through the rough spots. But remember, you must wield the power in your marriage judiciously. Flexibility and generosity are the signs of a secure and united couple.

Every life stage of a marriage has its own special issues, concerns, and milestones with which to contend. Through each of these phases, the influence of parents and in-laws will be felt and will need to be contained or modified. However, the tools required for this task remain the same no matter how long you are married. The skills revealed in this book will help you handle any situation that might arise along the way. It is through compassion, responsibility, and hard work that you can secure a fair and loving relationship with your parents and in-laws. When Robert Frost said that "The best way out is always through," he might have been speaking to couples facing these tasks. It is not useful to just hope that things will work out or that time will set things straight. A marriage that is strong and successful works hard at managing the influence of parents and in-laws upon it— working through and not skirting around difficult issues.

Every couple must decide for themselves how to interact with the world of family. There are no rules, no right way, to integrate parents and in-laws into a marriage. In fact, these relationships may be redefined and redesigned many times over the course of your marriage. It is imperative to remain open and flexible, as the years go by, to reinvent your relationship with your parents. As your marriage changes and evolves, so too will your parents develop and mature. There is always the possibility that at some time along the journey of your marriage you will be able to incorporate your parents and create a joyful extended family. Then you will feel the historic and timeless phenomenon of generations coming together. So the next time you and your spouse pass a mirror, have courage and examine your reflections carefully. In it you will find reflections of the past and future of your family and marriage. On it you will cast your own marital reflection, and proudly leave it as a legacy for your children to ponder when they consult the Marriage Mirror in years to come.

SOURCE NOTES

Introduction
1. Sontag, Susan. "In Plato's Cave," *On Photography*, 1977.
2. Mead, Margaret. *New Realities,* June 1978.
3. Emlen, Stephen T. and Peter H. Wrege. "Parent-Offspring Conflict and the Recruitment of Helpers Among Bee-Eaters," *Nature,* Vol. 356, March 26, 1992.
4. Salk, Dr. Lee. *Familyhood,* Simon and Schuster, NY, 1994, p. 148.

SECTION ONE: THE MARRIAGE MIRROR
Chapter One: Reflections
5. Pound, Ezra. "Affirmations—As for Imagisme," *Selected Prose 1909–65*, pt. 7 (ed. by William Cookson, 1973).

SECTION TWO: RENEGOTIATING ATTACHMENTS
Chapter Three: The Cast of Characters
6. Duvall, Evelyn Millis, Ph.D. *In-laws Pro and Con: An Original Study of Interpersonal Relations,* Associated Press, New York, 1954.
7. Frazer, James G. *The Golden Bough,* 1922 ed., ch. 18.

Chapter Four: The "Royal We" of Marriage
8. Jefferson, Thomas. First inaugural address, March 4, 1801.
9. Aeschylus. *Fragments* (525–456 BC).

Chapter Five: Coming to Consensus
10. Franklin, Benjamin. Comment heard at the signing of the Declaration of Independence, July 4, 1776.
11. Benson, Stella. *Pipers and a Dancer,* ch. 9, 1924.

Chapter Six: The Judicious Use of Power
12. Disraeli, Benjamin. *Sybil,* Book 4, ch. 14, 1845.
13. Laing, R. D. *The Self and Others,* ch. 10, 1961.
14. Yeats, W. B. *Easter,* 1916.
15. Collette. "The Priest on the Wall," *My Mother's House,* 1922.

SECTION THREE: THE MARRIAGE SAMPLER
16. Maurois, Andre. "The Art of Marriage," *The Art of Living,*
    1940.

Chapter Nine: The World of Work
17. Dos Passos, John. *The New York Times,* October 25, 1959.

Chapter Ten: Grandparents
18. King, Florence. *Reflections in a Jaundiced Eye,* 1989.

Chapter Eleven: Aging Parents—Family Helping Family
19. Rockefeller, John D. *Ten Principles,* Address on behalf of US
    organizations, NY, 1941.
20. Frost, Robert. *A Servant to Servants,* 1942.

ABOUT THE AUTHOR

NANCY WASSERMAN COCOLA, M.S.W., is a psychotherapist in private practice in Manhattan and Pawling, New York, working with individuals and couples as well as having a particular focus on mother/daughter and parenting issues. She is the coauthor of *How to Manage Your Mother: Skills and Strategies to Improve Mother-Daughter Relationships*, published by Simon and Schuster in 1992. A Literary Guild® alternate selection, her book was also published in Germany, China, Norway and Denmark.

Ms. Wasserman Cocola has appeared on *Oprah, Good Day New York,* and the *Sally Jessy Raphael* show. She lectures regularly to women's groups and civic organizations.

She graduated from the Hunter School of Social Work with a master's degree and then went on to the Gestalt Associates of New York, where she completed a four-year postgraduate program in Gestalt and Family Therapy. She taught individual and family therapy to physicians and social work graduate students during her nine-year tenure at The New York Hospital.

She is the cofounder of Partners In Education—a group designed to foster open communication and constructive dialogue between parents and educators. Ms. Wasserman Cocola lives in Pawling, New York, where she is the married mother of a ten-year-old son.